OLIVE OATMAN.

CAPTIVITY

OF THE

OATMAN GIRLS:

BEING AN

Interesting Narrative of Life

AMONG THE

APACHE AND MOHAVE INDIANS.

CAPTIVITY

OF THE

OATMAN GIRLS:

BEING AN

Interesting Narrative of Life

AMONG THE

APACHE AND MOHAVE INDIANS.

CONTAINING

AN INTERESTING ACCOUNT OF THE MASSACRE OF THE OATMAN FAMILY, BY THE APACHE INDIANS, IN 1851; THE NARROW ESCAPE OF LORENZO D. OATMAN; THE CAPTURE OF OLIVE A. AND MARY A. OATMAN; THE DEATH, BY STARVATION, OF THE LATTER; THE FIVE YEARS' SUFFERING AND CAPTIVITY OF OLIVE A. OATMAN; ALSO, HER SINGULAR RECAPTURE IN 1856; AS GIVEN BY LORENZO D. AND OLIVE A. OATMAN, THE ONLY SURVIVING MEMBERS OF THE FAMILY, TO THE AUTHOR.

R.B. STRATTON

TWENTIETH THOUSAND.

KALPAZ

ISBN: 978-93-5128-532-8

First Published in 1857
Indian Reprint in 2017

Published by

Kalpaz Publications
C-30, Satyawati Nagar,
Delhi – 110052
E-mail: kalpaz@hotmail.com
Website: kalpazpublications.com
Ph.: +91-9212142040

Cataloging in Publication Data—DK
Courtesy: D.K. Agencies (P) Ltd. <docinfo@dkagencies.com>

Stratton, R. B. (Royal Byron), 1827-1875, **author.**
Captivity of the Oatman girls : being an interesting narrative of life among the Apache and Mohave Indians / R.B. Stratton.
pages cm
"First published in 1857"—Title page verso.
ISBN 9789351285328

1. Indian captivities—Southwest, New. 2. Oatman, Olive Ann—Captivity, 1851. 3. Oatman, Mary Ann, -1852—Captivity, 1851. 4. Apache Indians. 5. Mohave Indians. 6. Oatman family. I. Title.

E99.A6S77 2017 DDC 979.1040922 23

PREFACE TO THE FIRST EDITION

During the year 1851 news reached California, that in the spring of that year a family by the name of OATMAN, while endeavoring to reach California by the old Santa Fe route, had met with a most melancholy and terrible fate, about seventy miles from Fort Yuma. That while struggling with every difficulty imaginable, such as jaded teams, exhaustion of their stores of provisions, in a hostile and barren region, alone and unattended, they were brutally set upon by a horde of Apache savages; that seven of the nine persons composing their family were murdered, and that two of the smaller girls were taken into captivity.

One of the number, LORENZO D. OATMAN, a boy about fourteen, who was knocked down and left for dead, afterward escaped, but with severe wounds and serious injury.

But of the girls, MARY ANN and OLIVE ANN, nothing had since been heard, up to last March. By a singular and mysteriously providential train of circumstances, it was ascertained at that time, by persons living at Fort Yuma, that one of these girls was then living among the Mohave tribe, about four hundred miles from the fort. A ransom was offered for her by the ever–to–be–remembered and generous Mr. GRINELL, then a mechanic at the fort; and through the agency and tact of a Yuma Indian, she was purchased and restored to civilized life, to her brother and friends. The younger of the girls, MARY ANN, died of starvation in 1852.

It is of the massacre of this family, the escape of LORENZO, and the captivity of the two girls, that the following pages treat.

A few months since the author of this book was requested by the afflicted brother and son, who barely escaped with life, but not without much suffering, to write the past history of the family; especially to give a full and particular account of the dreadful and barbarous scenes of the captivity endured by his sisters. This I have tried to do. The facts and incidents have been received from the brother and sister, now living.

These pages have been penned under the conviction that in these facts, and in the sufferings and horrors that befell that unfortunate family, there is sufficient of interest, though of a melancholy character, to insure an attentive and interested perusal by every one into whose hands, and under whose eye this book may fall. Though, so far as book–making is concerned, there has been brought to this task no experience or fame upon which to base an expectation of its popularity, yet the writer has sought to adapt the style to the character of the narrative, and in a simple, plain, comprehensive manner to give to the reader facts, as they have been received firom those of whose sad experiences in adversity these pages give a faithful delineation. In doing this he has sought plainness, brevity, and an unadorned style, deeming these the only excellences that could be appropriately adopted for such a narrative; the only ones that he expects will be awarded. It would be but a playing with sober, solemn, and terrible reality to put the tinselings of romance about a narrative of this kind. The intrinsic interest of the subject mnatter here thrown together, must have the credit of any circulation that shall be given to the book. Upon this I am willing to rely; and that it will be sufficient to procure a wide and general perusal, remunerating and exciting, I have the fullest confidence. As for criticisms, while there will, no doubt, be found occasions for them, they are neither coveted nor dreaded. All that is asked is, that the reader will avail himself of the facts, and dismiss, as far as he can, the garb they wear, for it was not woven by one who has ever possessed a desire to become experienced or skilled in that ringing, empty style which can only charm for the moment, and the necessity for which is never felt but when real matter and thought are absent.

That all, or any considerable portion, of the distress, mental and physical, that befell that unfortunate family, the living as well as dead, can be written or spoken, it would be idle to claim. The desolation and privation to which little MARY ANN was consigned while yet but seven years old; the abuse, the anguish, the suffering that rested upon the nearly two years' captivity through which she passed to an untimely grave; the unutterable anguish that shrouded with the darkness of despair five years of her older sister; the six years of perpetual tossing from transient hope to tormenting fears, and during which unceasing toil and endeavor was endured by the elder brother, who knew at that time, and has ever since known, that two of his sisters were taken into captivity by the Indians; these, all these are realities that are and must forever remain unwritten. We would not, if we could, give to these pages the power to lead the reader into all the paths of torture and woe through which the last five years have dragged that brother and sister, who yet live, and who, from hearts disciplined in affliction, have herein dictated all of what they have felt that can be transferred to the type. We would not, if we could, recall or hold up to the reader the weight of parental solicitude or heartyearnings for their dear family that crowded upon the last few moments of reason allowed to those fond parents, while in the power and under the war–clubs of their Apache murderers. The heart's deepest anguish, and its profoundest emotions have no language. There is no color so deep that pen dipped therein can portray the reality. If what may be here found written of these unspoken woes shall only lead the favored subjects of constant good fortune to appreciate their exempted allotment, and create in their hearts a more earnest and practical sympathy for those who tread the damp, uncheered paths of suffering and woe, then the moral and social use prayed for and intended in these pages will be secured.

YREKA, 1857. R. B. STRATTON.

PREFACE TO THE SECOND EDITION

SINCE issuing the first edition of the "CAPTIVITY OF THE OATMAN GIRLS," which obtained a rapid and quick sale, the author has been in the northern part of the state, busy with engagements made previous to its publication, and which he considered he had ample time to meet, and return before another edition would be called for, if at all. But in this he was mistaken. Only two weeks had elapsed before orders were in the city for books, that could not be filled; and that but a few days after the whole edition was bound. The first five thousand was put out as an experiment, and with considerable abridgment from the original manuscript as at first prepared. Considerable matter referring to the customs of the Indians, and the geography and character of the country, was left out to avoid the expense of publishing. Could we have known that the first edition would have been exhausted so soon, this omitted matter might have been re–prepared and put into this edition, but the last books were sold when the author was five hundred miles from his present home, and on returning it was thought best to hurry this edition through the press, to meet orders already on hand. We trust the reader will find most, if not all, of the objectionable portions of the first edition expunged from this; besides the insertion in their proper places of some additions that were, without intention, left out of the former one. He will also find this printed upon superior paper and type; and in many ways improved in its appearance.

We must remind the reader, that in preparing a work like the present there is an utter impropriety in resorting to any other than the plainest matter–of–fact style. This book is not a romance. It is not dependent upon an exorbitant fictitiousness of expression for enlisting the attention or interest of the sober reader. The scene is a reality. The heroes of the tale are living. Let those, if any there are, to whom reality is a serious obstacle to engaged and sustained attention and interest, and whose morbidly created taste, has given a settled disrelish for marvels in the facts, while it unceasingly clamors for miracles of the fancy; to whom plain things, said in a plain way, have no attraction, whose reading heaven is a mountain of epithet on flashing epithet piled–let such lay aside the book.

The writer does not disclaim literary taste. Such a taste it is confidently felt is not herein violated. For its display these pages are not intended. These remarks are here penned for the reason that in a few instances, instead of an open criticism, founded upon the reading of the book, there has been a construing of the frank avowel of the real intention of this book, made in a former preface, into a confession of a literary weakness in the composition of this work. The writer for the last eleven years has been engaged in public speaking, and though moving contentedly in an humble sphere, is not without living testimonials to his diligence and fidelity, at least in application to those literary studies and helps to his calling which were within his reach. With a present consciousness of many imperfections in this respect, he is nevertheless not forbidden by a true modesty to say, that in a laudable ambition to acquire and command the pure English, from the root upward, he has not been wholly negligent nor unsuccessful; nor in the habit of earnest and particular observation of men and things has he been without his note–book and open eyes.

During the years spoken of he has seldom appeared before the public without a carefully written compendium, and often a full manuscript of the train of thought to be discoursed upon.

But still, if his attainments were far more than are here claimed, it would by some be judged a poor place to use them for the feasting of the reader of a book of the nature of this record of murder, wailing, captivity, and horrid separations.

The notices in the papers referred to have, no doubt, grown from a habit that prevails to a great extent, of writing a notice of a new book from a hasty glance at a preface. Hence, he who can gyrate in a brilliant circle of polished braggadocio in his firstborn, is in a fair way to meet the echo of his own words, and be "puffed!"

But, unpretending as are these pages, the author, in his own behalf, and in behalf of those for and of whom he writes, is under many obligations to the press of the State. In many instances a careful perusal has preceded a public printed notice by an editor; and with some self–complacency he finds that such notices have been the most flattering and have done most to hasten the sale of these books.

The author, still making no pretensions to a serving up of a repast for the literary taste, yet with confidence assures the reader that he will find nothing upon these pages that can offend such a taste.

Let it be said further, that the profits accruing from the sale of this work are, so far as the brother and sister are concerned, to be applied to those who need help. It was with borrowed means that Mr. Oatman published the first edition, and it is to secure means to furnish himself and his sister with the advantages of that education which has been as yet denied, that the narrative of their five years' privation is offered to the reading public. Certainly, if the eye or thought delights not to wander upon the page of their sufferings, the heart will delight to think of means expended for the purchase of the book that details them.

SAN FRANCTSCO, 1857.

PREFACE TO THE THIRD EDITION

The second edition of this book (six thousand copies) was nearly exhausted in the California and Oregon trade within a few months after its publication. Numerous friends and relatives of Mr. and Miss Oatman, who had received copies of the work from friends in California, wrote to the writer, and also to the Oatmans, urgently requesting its publication for circulation in the Atlantic and Western States.

They had read the book, and loaned it to neighbors and friends, until each copy numbered a considerable circle of readers, and an almost unanimous opinion had been expressed that the book would meet with a large and ready sale if it could be put into the market at prices ruling on this side of the continent.

In behalf of those for whose special benefit the book is published, the writer can but feel grateful for the large sales that in a few weeks were effected in California. Eleven thousand were sold there in a short time, and the owner of the book has deeply regretted that it was not stereotyped at the first.

Recently, to meet demands for the book already existing, especially in some of the Western States, where the Oatman family were well known, it was resolved to publish the book in New–York, in an improved style, and with the addition of some incidents that were prepared for the California issue, but omitted from the necessity of the case.

The reader will find the book much improved in its intrinsic interest by the addition of these geographical, traditional, and historic items. The matter added is chiefly of the peculiar traditions and superstitions of the tribes who were the captors and possessors of Miss Oatman. Three new illustrations are also added, and the old ones newly drawn and engraved. Every plate has been enlarged, and the work done in a much improved and more perfect style.

The reader will find this book to be a record of facts; and these are of the most thrilling some of them of the most horrid nature. Of all the records of Indian captivities we feel confident none have possessed more interest than this. Numerous have been the testimonies from California readers that it exceeds any of kindred tales that have preceded it. The Oatman family were well and favorably known in portions of Illinois and Pennsylvania, and a large circle of acquaintances are waiting, with much anxiety, the issue from the press of this narrative of the tragical allotment that they met after starting for the Colorado in 1850. Seven of their number have fallen by the cruelties of the Indian; two, a brother and sister, are now in this city.

There are sketches and delineations in this volume touching the region lying to the West and Southwest, as also of the large aboriginal tribes that have so long held exclusive possession there, which, in these times of the unparalleled westward–pushing propensities of our people, are clothed with new and startling interest day by day.

In the purchase of this book the reader will add to his private or family library a volume whose chief attraction will not be merely in the detail of horrors, of suffering, of cruel captivity, which it brings to him; but one which his children will find valuable for reference in the years they may live to see, and which are to be crowded, doubtless, with an almost total revolution in the humanities that people the region lying between the Pacific and Texas, and between Oregon and Mexico. These dark Indian tribes are fast wasting before the rising sun of our civilization; and into that history that is yet to be written of their past, and of their destiny, and of the many interlacing events that are to contribute to the fulfilling of the wise intent of Providence concerning them and their only chdreaded foe, the white race, facts and incidents contained in this unpretending volume will enter and be appreciated.

New–York, April, 1858. R. B. STRATTON.

CONTENTS

Illustrations

MOHAVE
2d Captivity
MOHAVE R.
COLORADO R.
WILLIAMS FORK
CALIFORNIA
NEW MEXICO
1st Captivity
TOUTO APACHES
SAN FRANCISCO R.
SALINA RIVER
RUINS
RUINS
YUMAS
COLORADO R.
GILA RIVER
Indian Village
PLACE OF MASACRE
FORT YUMAS
GILA RIVER
GADSDEN PURCHASE
SAN PEDRO R.
LOWER CAL.
COCOPAS
SONORA
34
33
114
113
112
111

CHAPTER I

The first Encampment–The Oatman Family–Their checkered Allottment up to the Time of their Emigration–Mr. Oatman–His Ill–health–Proposes to join the Party organized to form an American Colony near the Gulf of California, in 1849–The 10th of August–Discord in Camp, owing to the religious Prejudices of a few–First Danger from Indians–The Camanche Band–Two Girls taken for "Injins–The Grape Dumpling–Mexican Settlements–The Hunt for Antelopes, and its tragical End–Charles refuscs to fight "Iinjins"' with Prayer–Moro–Scarcity of Provisions–Discontent and Munriurings–Mr. Lane–His Death–Loss of Animals by the Apaches —Mrs. M. in the Well–Santa Cruz and Tukjon–Some of the Company remain here Pimiole–The only traveling Companions of the Oatman Family resolve to remain–Mr. Oatman, in Perplexity, resolves to proceed.

The 9th of August, 1850, was a lovely day. The sun had looked upon the beautiful plains surrounding Independence, Missouri, with a full, unclouded face, for thirteen hours of that day; when, standing about four miles south of westward from the throbbing city of Independence, alive with the influx and, efflux of emigrant men and women, the reader, could he have occupied that stand, might have seen, about one half hour before sunset, an emigrant train slowly approaching him from the city. This train consisted of about twenty wagons, a band of emigrant cattle, and about fifty souls, men, women, and children. Attended by the music of lowing cattle, and the chatter of happy children, it was slowly traversing a few miles, at this late hour of the day, to seek a place of sufficient seclusion to enable them to hold the first and preparatory night's camp away from the bustle and confusion of the town.

Just as the sun was gladdening the clear west, and throwing its golden farewells upon the innumerable peaks that stretched into a forest of mountains gradually rising until they seemed to lean against the sunclad shoulders of the Rocky Range, imparadising the whole plain and mountain country in its radiant embrace, the shrill horn of the leader and captain suddenly pealed through the moving village, a circle was formed, and the heads of the several families were in presence of the commander, waiting orders for the camping arrangements for the night.

Soon teams were detached from the wagons, and with the cattle (being driven for commencement in a new country) were turned forth upon the grass. Rich and abundant pasturage was stretchling from the place of their halt westward, seemingly until it bordered against the foot–hills of the Indian territory in the distance.

Among the fifty souls that composed that emigrant band, some were total strangers. Independence had been selected as the gatherinig–place of all who might heed a call that had been published and circulated for months, beating up for volunteers to an emigrant company about seeking a home in the Southwest. It was intended, as the object and destination of this company, to establish an American colony near the mouth of the Gulf of California. Inducements had been held out, that if the region lying about the juncture of the Colorado and Gila Rivers could thus be colonized, every facility should be guaranteed the colonists for making to themselves a comfortable and luxuriant home.

After a frugal meal, served throughout the various divisions of the camp, the evening of the 9th was spent in perfecting regulations for the long and dangerous trip, and in the formning of acquaintances, and the interchange of salutations and gratulations.

Little groups, now larger and now smaller, by the constant moving to and fro of members of the camp, had chatted the evening up to a seasonable bedtime. Then, at the call of the "crier," all were collected around one camp–fire for the observance of public worship, which was conducted by a clergyman present. Into that hour of earnest worship were crowded memories of the

First Night's Encampment.

home–land and friends now forever abandoned for a settlement in the "far–off Southwest." There flowed and mingled the tear of regret and of hope; there and then rose the earnest prayer for Providential guidance; and at that hour there swelled out upon the soft, clear air of as lovely al evening as ever threw its star–lit curtain upoin hill and vale, the song of praise and thie shout of triumpl, not alone in the prospect of a home by the Colorado of the South, but of glad exultation in the prospect of a home hard by the' "River of Life," which rose to view as the final termination of the journeyings and toil incident to mortality's pilgrimage.

Now the hush of sleep's wonted hour has stolen slowly over the entire encampment, and nothing without indicates remaining life, save the occasional growl of the ever–faithful watch–dog, or the outburst of some infant member of that villa–camp, wearied and worn, and overtasked by the hurry and bustle of the previous day.

Reader, we now wish you to go with us into that camp, and receive an introduction to an interesting family consisting of father, mother, and seven children; the oldest of this juvenile group a girl of sixteen, the youngest a bright little boy of one year. Silence is here, but to that household sleep has no welcome. The giant undertaking upon which they are now fairly launched is so freighted with interest to themselves and their little domestic kingdom, as to leave no hour during the long night for the senses to yield to the soft dominion of sleep. Besides, this journey now before them has been preceded by lesser ones, and these had been so frequent and of such trivial result as that vanity seemed written upon all the deep and checkered past, with its world of toil and journeyings. In a subdued whisper, but with speaking countenances and sparkling eyes, these parents are dwelling upon this many–colored by–gone.

Mr. Oatman is a medium–sized man, about five feet in height, black hair, with a round face, and yet in the very prime of life. Forty–one winters had scarcely been able to plow the first furrow of age upon his manly cheek. Vigorous, healthy, and of a jovial turn of mind, predisposed to look only upon the bright side of everything, he was happy; of a sanguine temperament, he was given to but little fear, and seemed ever drinking from the fresh fountains of a living buoyant hope. From his boyhood he had been of a restless, roving disposition, fond of novelty, and anxious that nothing within all the circuit of habitable earth should be left out of the field of his ever curious and prying vision.

He had been favored with rare educational advantages during his boyhood, in Western New–York. These advantages he had improved with a promising vigilance until about nineteen years of age. He then became anxious to see, and try his fortune in, the then far away West. The thought of emigrating had not been long cogitated by his quick and ready mind, ere he came to a firm resolution to plant his feet upon one of the wild prairies of Illinois.

He was now of age, and his father and mother, Lyman and Lucy Oatman, had spent scarcely one year keeping hotel in Laharpe, Illinois, ere they were joined by their son Royse.

Soon after going to Illinois, Royse was joined in marriage to Miss Mary Ann Sperry, of Laharpe. Miss Sperry was an intelligent girl of about eighteen, and, by nature and educational advantages, abundantly qualified to make her husband happy and his home an attraction. She was sedate, confiding, and affectionate, and in social accomplishments placed by her peculiar advantages, above most of those around her. From childhood she had been the pride of fond and wealthy parents; and it was their boast that she had never merited a rebuke for any wrong. The first two years of this happy couple was spent on a farm near Laharpe. During this time some little means had been accumulated by an honest industry and economy, and these means Mr. Oatman collected, and with them embarked in mercantile business in Laharpe.

Honesty, industry, and a number of years of thorough business application, won for him the esteem of those around him, procured a comfortable home for his family, and placed him in possession of a handsome fortune, with every arrangement for its rapid increase. At that time the country was rapidly filling up; farmers were becoming rich, and substantial improvements were taking the place of temporary modes of living which had prevailed as yet.

Paper money became plenty, the products of the soil had found a ready and remunerative market, and many were induced to invest beyond their means in real estate improvements.

The banks chartered about the years 1832 and 1840, had issued bills beyond their charters, presuming upon the continued rapid growth of the country to keep themselves above disaster. But business, especially in times of speculation, like material substance, is of a gravitating tendency, and without a basis soon falls. A severe reverse in the tendency of the markets spread rapidly over the entire West during the year 1842. Prices of produce fell to a low figure. An abundance had been raised, and the market was glutted. Debts of long standing became due, and the demand for their payment became more imperative, as the inability of creditors became more and more apparent and appalling. The merchant found his store empty his goods having been credited to parties whose sole reliance was the usual ready market for the products of their soil.

Thus, dispossessed of goods and destitute of money, the trading portion of community were thrown into a Peni, and business of all kinds came to a standstill. The producing classes were straitened; their grain would not meet current expenses, for it had no market value; and with many of them mortgages, bearing high interest, were preying like vultures upon their already declining realities.

Specie was scarce. Bills were returned to the banks, and while a great many of them were yet out the specie was exhausted, and a general crash came upon the banks, while the country was yet flooded with what was appropriately termed "the wild–cat money." The day of reckoning to these spurious money fountains suddenly weighed them in the balances and found them wanting. Mr. Oatman had collected in a large amount of this paper currency, and was about to go South to replenish his mercantile establishment, when lo! the banks began to fail, and in a few weeks he found himself sunk by the weight of several thousands into utter insolvency.

He was disappointed but not disheartened. To him a reverse was the watchword for a renewal of energy. For two or three years he had been in correspondence with relatives residing in Cumberland Valley, Pennsylvania, who had been constantly holding up that section of country as one of the most inviting and desirable for new settlers.

In a few weeks he had disposed of the fragments of a suddenly shattered fortune to the greatest possible advantage to his creditors, and resolved upon an immediate removal to that valley. In two months preparations were made, and in three months, with a family of five children, he arrived among his friends in Cumberland Valley, with a view of making that a permanent settlement.

True to the domineering traits of his character, he was still resolute and undaunted. His wife was the same trusting, cheerful companion as when the nuptial vow was plighted, and the sun of prosperity shone full upon and crowned their mutual toils. Retired, patient, anld persevering, she was a faithful wife and a fond mother, in whom centered deservingly the love of a growing and interesting juvenile group. She became more and more endeared to her fortune taunted husband as adverse vicissitudes had developed her real worth, and her full competence to brave and profit by the stern battles of life.

She had seen her husband when prospered, and flattered by those whose attachments had taken root in worldly considerations only; she had stood by him also when the chilling gusts of temporary adversity had blown the cold damps of cruel reserve and fiendish suspicion about his name and character; and

> "When envy's sneer would coldly blight his name,
> And busy tongues were sporting with his fame,
> She solved each doubt, and clear'd each mist away,
> And made him radiant in the face of day."

They had spent but a few months in Pennsylvania, the place of their anticipated abode for life, ere Mr. Oatman found it, to him, an unfit and unsuitable place, as also an unpromising region in which to rear a family. He sighed again for the wide, wild prairie lands of the West. Hie began to regret that a financial reversion should have been allowed so soon to drive him from a country where he had been accustomed to behold the elements and foundation of a glorious and prosperous future; and where those very religious and educational advantages–to him the indispensable accompaniments of social progress were already beginning to shoot forth in all the vigor and promise of a healthful and undaunted growth. He was not of that class who can persist in an enterprise merely from pride that is so weak as to scorn the confession of a weakness; though he was slow to change his purpose, only as a good reason might dis cover itself under the light and teachings of multi plying circumstances around him.

He resolved to retrace his steps, and again to try his hands and skill upon some new and unbroken portion of the State where he had already made and lost. Early in 1845 these parents, with a family of five children, destitute but courageous, landed in Chicago. There, for one year, they supported with toil of head and hand (the father was an experienced school teacher) their growing family.

In the spring of 1846 there might have been seen standing, at about five miles from Fulton, Ill., and about fifteen from New–Albany, alone in the prairie, a temporary, rude cabin. Miles of unimproved land stretched away on either side, save a small spot, rudely fenced, near the cabin, as the commencement of a home. At the door of this tent, in April of'that year, and about sunset, a wagon drawn by oxen, and driven by the father of a family, a man about thirty–seven, and his son, a lad about ten years, halted. That wagon contained a mother–a woman of thirty–three years–toil–worn but contented, with five of her children. The oldest son, Lorenzo, who had been plodding on at the father's side, dragged his weary limbs up to the cabin door, and begged admittance for the night. This was readily and hospitably granted. Soon the family were transported from the movable to the staid habitation. Here they rested their stomachs upon "Johnny cake" and Irish potatoes, and their weary, complaining bodies upon the soft side of a white oak board for the night.

Twenty–four hours had not passed ere the father had staked out a "claim;" a tent had been erected; the cattle turned forth, were grazing upon the hitherto untrodden prairie land, and preparations made and measures put into vigorous operation for spring sowing. Here, with that same elasticity of mind and prudent energy that had inspired his earliest efforts for self–support, Mr. Oatman commenced to provide himself a home, and to surround his family with all the comforts and conveniences of a subsistence. Before his energetic and well–directed endeavors, the desert soon began to blossom; and beauty and fruitfulness gradually stole upon these hitherto wild and useless regions. He always managed to provide his family with a plain, frugal, and plenteous support.

Four years and over Mr. and Mrs. Oatman toiled early and late, clearing, subduing, and improving. And during this time they readily and cheerfully turned their hands to any laudable calling, manual or intellectual, that gave promise of a just remuneration for their services. Althou,gh accustomed, for the most part of their united life, to a competence that had placed them above the necessity of menial service, yet they scorned a dependence upon past position, as also that pride and utter recklessness of principle which can consent to keep up the exterior of opulence, while its expenses must come fiom unsecured and deceived creditors. They contentedly adapted themselves to a manner and style that was intended to give a true index to their real means and resources.

It was this principle of noble self–reliance, and unbending integrity, that won for them the warmest regards of the good, and crowned their checkered allotment with appreciative esteem wherever their stay had been sufficient to make them known.

While the family remained at this place, now called Henly, they toiled early and late, at home or abroad, as opportunity might offer. During much of this time, however, Mr. Oatman was laboring under and battling with a serious bodily infirmity and indisposition.

Early in the second year of their stay at Henly, while lifting a stone, in digging a well for a neighbor, he injured himself, and from the effects of that injury he never fully recovered.

At this time improvements around him had been conducted to a stage of advancement that demanded a strict and vigilant oversight and guidance. And though by these demands, and his unflagging ambition, he was impelled to constant, and at times to severe labors, yet they were labors for which he had been disabled, and from which he should have ceased. Each damp or cold season of the year, after receiving this injury to his back and spine, would place him upon a rack of pain, and at times render life a torture. The winters, always severe in that section of the country, that had blasted and swept away frailer constitutions about him, had as yet left no discernible effects upon his vigorous physical system. But now their return almost disabled him for work, and kindled anew the torturing local inflammation that his injury had brought with it to his system.

He became convinced that if he would live to bless and educate his family, or would enjoy even tolerable health, he must immediately seek a climate free from the sudden and extreme changes so common to the region in which he had spent the last few years.

In the summer of 1849 an effort was made to induce a party to organize, for the purpose of emigration to that part of the New–Mexican Territory lying about the mouth of the Rio Colorado and Gila Rivers. Considerable excitement extended over the northern and western portions of Illinois concerning it. There were a few men, men of travel and information, who were well acquainted with the state of the country lying along the east side of the northern end of the Gulf of California, and they had received the most flattering inducements to form there a colony of the Anglo–Saxon people.

Accordingly notices were circulated of the number desired and of the intention and destiny of the undertaking. The country was represented as of a mild, bland climate, where the extremes of a hot summer and severe winter were unknown. Mr. Oatman, after considerable deliberation upon the state of his health, the necessity for a change of climate, the reliability of the information that had come from this new quarter, and other circumstances having an intimate connection with the welfare of those dependent upon him, sent in his name, as one who, with a family, nine in all, was ready to join the colony; and again he determined to attempt his fortune in a new land.

He felt cheered in the prospect of a location where he might again enjoy the possibility of a recovery of his health. And he hoped that the journey itself might aid the return of his wonted vigor and strength.

After he had proposed a union with this projected colony, and his proposition had been favorably received, he immediately sold out. The sum total of the sales of his earthly possessions amounted to fifteen hundred dollars. With this he purchased an outfit, and was enabled to reserve to himself sufficient, as he hoped, to meet all incidental expenses of the tedious trip.

In the spring of 1850, accompanied by some of his neighbors, who had also thrown their lots into this scheme, he started for Independence, the place selected for the gathering of the scattered members of the colony, preparatory to a united travel for the point of destination. Every precaution had been taken to secure unanimity of feeling, purpose, and intention among those who should propose to cast in their lot with the emigrating colony. All were bound for the same place; all were inspired by the same object; all should enter the band on an equality; and it was agreed that every measure of importance to the emigrant army, should be brought to the consideration and consultation of every member of the train.

It was intended to form a new settlement, remote from the prejudices, pride, arrogance, and caste that obtain in the more opulent and less sympathizing portions of a stern civilization. Many of the number thought they saw in the locality selected many advantages that were peculiar to it alone. They looked upon it as the way by which emigration would principally reach this western gold–land, furnishing for the colony a market for their produce; that thus remote they could mold, fashion, and direct the education, habits, customs, and progress of the young and growing colony, after a model superior to that under which some of them had been discontentedly raised, and one that should receive tincture, form, and adaptation from the opening and multiply ing necessities of the experiment in progress.

As above stated, this colony, composed of more than fifty souls, encamped on the lovely evening of August 9, 1850, about four miles from Independence.

The following are the names of those who were the most active in projecting the movement, and their names are herein given, because they may be again alluded to in the following pages; besides, many of them are now living, and this may be the first notice they shall receive of the fate of the unfortunate family, the captivity and sufferings of the only two surviving members of which are the themes of these pages. Mutual perils and mutual adventures have a power to cement worthy hearts that is not found in unmingled prosperity. And it has been the privilege of the author to know, from personal acquaintance, in one instance, of a family to whom the " Oatman Family" were bound by the tie of mutuality of suffering and geniality of spirit. Mr. Ira Thompson and family.

A. W. Lane and family.
R. and John Kelly and their families.
Mr. Mutere and family.
Mr. Wilder and family.
Mr. Brinshall and family.

We have thus rapidly sketched the outlines of the history of the Oatman family, for a few years preceding their departure from the eastern side of the continent, and glanced at the nature and cast of their allotment, because of members of that family these pages are designed mainly to treat. This remove, the steps to which have been traced above, proved their last; for though bright, and full of promise and hope, at the outset, tragedy of the most painful and gloomy character settles down upon it at an early period, and with fearfully portentous gloom, thickens and deepens upon its every step, until the day, so bright at dawn, gradually closes in all the horror and desolation of a night of plunder, murder, and worse than murderous and barbarous captivity. And though no pleasant task to bring this sad afterpart to the notice of the reader, it is nevertheless a tale that may be interesting for him to ponder; and instructive, as affording matter for the employment of reflection, and instituting a heartier sympathy with those upon whose life the clouds and pangs of severe reverses and misfortunes have rested.

Ere yet twilight had lifted the deepest shades of night from plain and hill–side, on the morning of the 10th of August, 1850, there was stir and bustle, and hurrying to and fro throughout that camp. As beautiful a sunrise as ever mantled the east, or threw its first, purest glories upon a long and gladdened West, found all things in order, and that itinerant colony arranged, prepared, and in march for the "Big Bend" of the Arkansas River. Their course at first lay due west, toward the Indian territory. One week passed pleasantly away. Fine weather, vigorous teams, social, cheerful chit–chat, in which the evenings were passed by men, women, aid children, who had been thrown into their first acquaintance under circumstances so well calculated to create identity of interest and aim, all contributed to the comfort of this anxious company during the " first week upon the plains," and to render the prospect for the future free from the first tint of evil adversity. At the end of a week, and when they had made about one hundred miles, a halt was called at a place known as the "Council Grove." This place is on the old Santa F6 road, and is well suited for a place of rest, and for recruiting. Up to this time naught but harmony and good feeling prevailed throughout the ranks of this emigrant company. While tarrying at this place, owing to the peculiarities in the religious notions and prejudices of a few restless spirits, the first note of discord and jarring element was introduced among them.

Some resolved to return, but the more sober (and such seemed in the majority) persisted in the resolve to accomplish the endeared object of the undertaking. Owing to their wise counsels, and moderate, dignified management, peace and quiet returned; and after a tarry of about one week's duration, they were again upon their journey. From Council Grove the road bore a little south of west, over a beautiful level plain, covered with the richest pasturage; and in the distance bordering on every hand against high, picturesque ranges of mountains, seeming like so many huge blue bulwarks, and forming natural boundaries between the abodes of the respective races, each claiming, separately and apart, the one the mountain, the other the vale.

The weather was beautiful; the evenings, cool and invigorating, furnishing to the jaded band a perfect elysium for the recruiting of tired nature, at the close of each day's sultry and dusty toil. Good feeling restored, all causes of irritation shut out, joyfully, merrily, hopefully, the pilgrim band moved on to the Big Bend, on the Arkansas River. Nothing as yet had been met to excite fear for personal safety; nothing to darken for a moment the cloudless prospect that had inspired and shone upon their first westward movings.

"It was our custom," says Lorenzo Oatman, " to lay by on the Sabbath, both to rest physical nature, and also, by proper religious services, to keep alive in our minds the remembrance of our obligations to our great and kind Creator and Preserver, and to remind ourselves that we were each travelers upon that great level of time, to a bourne from whence no traveler returns."

One Saturday night the tents were pitched upon the hither bank of the Arkansas River. On the next morning Divine service was conducted in the usual manner, and at the usual hour. Scarcely had the service terminated ere a scene was presented calculated to interrupt the general monotony, as well as awaken some not very agreeable apprehensions for their personal safety. A Mr. Mutere was a short way from the camp, on the other side of the river, looking after the stock. While standing and gazing about him, the sound of crude, wild music broke upon his ear. He soon perceived it proceeded from a band of Indians, whom he espied dancing and singing in the wildest manner in a grove near by. They were making merry, as if in exultation over some splendid victory. He soon ascertained that they were of the Camanche tribe, and about them were a number of very beautiful American horses and mules. He knew them to be stolen stock, from the saddle and harness marks, yet fresh and plainly to be seen. While Mr. Mutere stood looking at them his eye suddenly fell upon a huge, hideous looking "buck," partly concealed behind a tree, out from which he was leveling a gun at himself. He sprang into a run, much frightened, and trusted to leg bail for a safe arrival at camp.

At this the Indian came out, hallooed to Mutere, and made the most vehement professions of friendship, and of the absence of all evil design toward him. But Mutere chose not to tarry for any reassurance of his kindly interest in his welfare. As soon as Mutere was in camp, several Indians appeared upon the opposite side of the river, hallooing, and asking the privilege of coming into camp, avowing friendliness. After a little their request was granted, and about a score of them came up near the camp. The party soon had occasion to mark their folly in yielding to the request of the Indians, who were not long in their vicinity ere they were observed in secret council a little apart, also at the same time bending their bows and making ready their arrows, as if upon the eve of some malicious intent. "At this," says L. Oatman, "our boys were instantly to their guns, and upon the opposite side of the wagon, preparing them for the emergence. But we took good care to so hide us, as to let our motions plainly appear to the enemy, that they might take warning from our courage and not be apprised of our fears. Our real intention was immediately guessed at, as we could see by the change in the conduct of our new enemy. They, by this time, lowered their bows, and their few guns, and modestly made a request for a cow. This roused our resolution, and the demand was quickly resisted. We plainly saw unmistakable signs of fear, and a suspicion that they were standing a poor show for cow–beef from that quarter. Such was the first abrupt close that religious services had been brought to on our whole route as yet. These evil–designing wretches soon made off, with more dispatch evidently than was agreeable. A few hours after they again appeared upon the opposite bank, with about a score of fine animals, which they drove to water in our sight. As soon as the stock had drank, they raised a whoop, gave us some hearty cheering, and were away to the south at a tremendous speed. On Monday we crossed the river, and toward evening met a government train, who had been out to the fort and were now on their return. We related to them what we had seen. They told us that they had, a day or two before, come upon the remnant of a government train who were on their way to the fort, that their stock had been taken from them, and they were left in distress, and without means of return. They also informed us that during the next day we would enter upon a desert, where for ninety miles we would be without wood and water. This information, though sad, was timely. We at once made all possible preparations to traverse this old'Sahara' of the Santa Fd road. But these preparations as to water proved unnecessary, for while we were crossing this desolate and verdureless waste, the kindly clouds poured upon us abundance of fresh water, and each day's travel for this ninety miles was as pleasant as any of our trip to us, though to the stock it was severe."

While at the camp on the river one very tragical (?) event occurred, which must not be omitted. One Mr. M. A. M., Jun., had stepped down to the river bank, leisurely whistling along his way, in quest of a favorable place to draw upon the Arkansas for a pail of water. Suddenly two small girls, who had been a little absent from camp, with aprons upon their heads, rose above a little mound, and presented themselves to his view. His busy brain must have been preoccupied with "Injins," for the soon came running, puffing, and yelling into camp. As he went headlong over the wagon–tongue, his tin pail as it rolled starting a half–score of dogs to their feet, and setting them upon a yell, he lustily, and at the topmost pitch of voice, cried, " Injins! Injins!" He soon recovered his wits, however, and the pleasant little lasses came into camp with a hearty laugh that they had so unexpectedly been made the occasion of a rich piece of "fun."

From the river bend or crossing, on to Moro, the first settlement we reached in New Mexico, was about five hundred miles. During this time nothing of special interest occurred to break the almnost painful monotony of our way, or ruffle the quiet of our sociale, save an occasional family jar, the frequent crossing of pointed opinions, the now–and–then prophecies of "Injins ahead," etc., except one "Grape Dumpling" affair, which must be related by leaving a severe part untold. At one of our camps, on one of those fine water–courses that frequently set upon our way, from the mountains, we suddenly found ourselves near neighbors to a bounteously burdened grape orchard. Of these we ate freely. One of our principal and physically talented matrons, however, like the distrustful Israelites, determined not to trust to tomorrow for to–morrow's manna. She accordingly laid in a more than night's supply. The over–supply was, for safe keeping, done up "brown," in the form of well–prepared and thoroughly–cooked dumplings, and these deposited in a cellar–like stern end of the "big wagon." Unfortunate woman! if she had only performed these hiding ceremonies when the lank eye of one of our invalids, (?) Mr. A. P., had been turned the other way, she might have prevented a calamity, kindred to that which befell the ancient emigrants when they sought to lay by more than was demanded by immediate wants.

Now this A. P. had started out sick, and since his restoration had been constantly beleaguered by one of those dubious blessings, common as vultures upon the plains, a voracious appetite, an appetite that, like the grave, was constantly receiving yet never found a place to say, "Enough." Slowly he crawled from his bed, after he was sure that sleep had made Mrs. M. oblivious of her darling dumplings, and the rest of the camp unheedful of his movements, and, standing at the stern of the wagon, he deliberately emptied almost the entire contents of this huge dumpling pan into his ever–craving interior.

It seems that they had been safely stored in the wagon by this provident matron, to furnish a feast for the passengers when their travels might be along some grapeless waste; and but for the unnatural cravings of the unregulated appetite of A. P., might still have remained for that purpose. It was evident the next day that the invalid had been indulging in undue gluttony. He was "sick again," and, to use his own phrase, "like all backsliders, through worldly or stomach prosperity and repletion."

Madam M. now seized a stake, and thoroughly caned him through the camp, until dumpling strength was low, very low in the market.

After crossing the big desert, one day, while traveling, some of our company had their notions of our personal safety suddenly revolutionized under the following circumstances. A Mr. J. Thompson and a young man, C. M., had gone one side of the road some distance, hunting antelope. Among the hills, and when they were some distance in advance of the camp, they came upon a large drove of antelopes. They were ignorant at the time of their whereabouts, and the routed game started directly toward the train; but, to the hunters, the train seemed to be in directly the opposite direction. In the chase the antelopes soon came in sight of the train, and several little girls and boys, seeing them, and seeing their pursuers, ran upon a slight elevation to frighten the antelopes back upon the hunters; whereupon, by some unaccountable mirage deception, these little girls and boys were suddenly transformed into huge Indians to the eyes of the hunters. They were at once forgetful of their anticipated game, and regarding themselves as set upon by a band of some giant race, began to devise for their own escape. Mr. T., thinking that no mortal arm could rescue them, turned at once, and with much perturbation, to the young man, and vehemently cried out: " Charles, let us pray." Said Charles, "No, I'll be d—d if I'll pray; let us run;" and at this he tried the valor of running. All the exhortations of the old man to Charles "to drop his gun" were as fruitless as his entreaties to prayer. But when Mr. T. saw that Charles was making such rapid escape, he dropped his notions of praying, and took to the pursuit of the path left by the running but unpraying Charles. He soon outstripped the young man, and made him beg most lustily of the old man "to wait, and not run away and leave him there with the Injins alone."

The chagrin of the brave hunters, after they had reached camp by a long and circuitous route, may well be imagined, when they found that they had been running from their own children; and that their fright, and the running and fatigue it had cost them, had been well understood by those of the camp who had been the innocent occasion of their chase for antelopes suddenly being changed into a flight from "Injins."

When we came into the Mexican settlements our store of meats was well–nigh exhausted, and we were gratefully surprised to find that at every stopping place abundance of mutton was in market, fresh, and of superior quality, and to be purchased at low rates. This constituted our principal article of subsistence during the time we were traversing several hundred miles in this region.

Slowly, but with unmistakable indications of a melancholy character, disaffection and disorder crept into our camp. Disagreements had occurred among families. Those who had taken the lead in originating the project had fallen under the ban and censure of those who, having passed the novelty of the trip, were beginning to feel the pressure of its dark, unwelcome, and unanticipated realities. And, in some instances, a conduct was exhibited by those whose years and rank, as well as professions made at the outset, created expectation and confidence that in them would be found benefactors and wise counselors, that tended to disgrace their position, expose the unworthiness of their motives, and blast the bright future that seemed to hang over the first steps of our journeyings. As a consequence, feelings of discord were engendered, which gained strength by unwise and injudicious counsels, until their pestilential effects spread throughout the camp.

At Moro we tarried one night. This is a small Mexican town, of about three hundred inhabitants, containing, as the only objects of interest, a Catholic Mission station, now in a dilapidated state; a Fort, well–garrisoned by Mexican soldiers, and a fine stream of water, that comes, cool and clear, bounding down the mountain side, beautifying and reviving this finely located village.

The next day after leaving this place we came to the Natural, or Santa Fe Pass, and camped that night at the well–known place called the Forks. From this point there is one road leading in a more southerly direction, and frequently selected by emigrants after arriving at the Forks, though the other road is said, by those best acquainted, to possess many advantages. At this place we found that the disaffection, which had appeared for some time before, was growing more and more incurable; and it began to break out into a general storm. Several of our number resolved upon taking the south road; but this resolution was reached only as a means of separating themselves from the remainder of the train; for the intention really was to become detached from the restraints and counsels that they found interfering with their uncontrollable selfishness. There seemed to be no possible method by which these disturbing elements could be quelled, The matter gave rise to an earnest consultation and discussion upon the part of the sober and prudent portion of our little band; but all means and measures proposed for an amicable adjustment of variances and divisions, seemed powerless when brought in contact with the unmitigated selfishness that, among a certain few, had blotted out from their view the one object and system of regulation that they had been instrumental in throwing around the undertaking at first.

We now saw a sad illustration of the adage that "it is not all gold that glitters." The novelty of the scene, together with every facility for personal comfort and enjoyment, may suffice to spread the glad light of good cheer about the first few days or weeks of an emigrating tour upon these dreary plains; but let its pathway be found among hostile tribes for a number of weeks; let a scarcity of provisions be felt; let teams begin to fail, with no time or pasturage to recruit them; let inclement weather and swollen streams begin to hedge up the way; these, and more that frequently becomes a dreadful reality, have at once a wonderful power to turn every man into a kingdom by himself, and to develop the real nature of the most hidden motives of his being.

Several of those who had, with unwonted diligence and forbearance, sought to restore quiet and satisfaction, but to no purpose, resolved upon remaining here until the disaffected portion had selected the direction and order of their own movements, and then quietly pursue their way westward by the other route. After some delay, and much disagreeable discussion among themselves, the northern route was selected by the malcontents, and they commenced their travels apart. The remainder of us started upon the south road; and though our animals were greatly reduced, our social condition was greatly improved.

We journeyed on pleasantly for about one hundred miles, when we reached Socoro, a beautiful and some what thrifty Mexican settlement. Our teams were now considerably jaded, and we found it necessary to make frequent halts and tarryings for the purpose of recruiting them. And this we found it the more difficult to do, as we were reaching a season of the year, and section of country, that furnished a scanty supply of feed. We spent one week at Socoro, for the purpose of rest to ourselves and teams, as also to replenish, if possible, our fast diminishing store of supplies. We found that food was becoming more scarce among the settlements that lay along our line of travel; that quality and price were likewise serious difficulties, and that our wherewith to purchase even these was well–nigh exhausted.

We journeyed from Socoro to the Rio Grande amid many and disheartening embarrassments and troubles. Sections of the country were almost barren; teams were failing, and indications of hostility among the tribes of Indians (representatives of whom frequently gave us the most unwelcome greetings) were becoming more frequent and alarming.

Just before reaching the Rio Grande, two fine horses were stolen from Mr. Oatmnan. We afterward learned that they had been soon after seen among the Mexicans, though by them the theft was attributed to unfriendly neighboring tribes; and it was asserted that horses, stolen from trains of emigrants, were frequently brought into Mexican settlements and offered for sale. It is proper here to apprise the reader, that the project of a settlement in NewMexico had now been entirely abandoned since the division mentioned above, and that California had become the place where we looked for a termination of our travel, and the land where we hoped soon to reach and find a home. At the Rio Grande we rested our teams one week, as a matter of necessary mercy, for every day we tarried was only increasing the probability of the exhaustion of our provisions, ere we could reach a place of permnanent supply. We took from this point the "Cook and Kearney" route, and found the grass for our teams for a while more plentiful than for hundreds of miles previous. Our train now consisted of eight wagons and twenty persons. We now came into a mountainous country, and we found the frequent and severe ascents and declivities wearing upon our teams beyond any of our previous travel. We often consumed whole days in making less than one quarter of the usual day's advance. A few days after leaving the Rio Grande, one Mr. Lane died of the mountain fever. He was a man highly esteemed among the members of the train, and we felt his loss severely. We dug a grave upon one of the foot hills, and with appropriate funeral obsequies we lowered his remains into the same. Some of the female members of our company planted a flower upon the mound that lifted itself over his lonely grave. A rude stake, with his name and date of his death inscribed upon it, was all we left to mark the spot of his last resting–place. One morning, after spending a cool night in a bleak and barren place, we awoke with several inches of snow lying about us upon the hills in the distance. We had spent the night and a part of the previous day without water. Our stock were scattered during the night, and our first object, after looking them up, was to find some friendly place where we might slake our thirst.

The morning was cold, with a fierce bleak wind setting in from the north. Added to the pains of thirst, was the severity of the cold. We found that the weather is subject, in this region, to sudden changes, from one to the other extreme. While in this distressed condition some of our party espied in the distance a streak of timber letting down from the mountains, indicative of running living water. To go to this timber we immediately made preparation, with the greatest possible dispatch, as our only resort. And our half–wavering expectations were more than realized; for after a most fatiguing trip of nearly a day, during which many of us were suffering severely from thirst, we reached the place, and found not only timber and water in abundance, but a plentiful supply of game. Turkeys, deer, antelope, and wild sheep were dancing through every part of the beautiful woodland that lured us from our bleak mountain camp. As the weather continued extremely cold we must have suffered severely, if we had not lost our lives, even, by the severity of the weather, as there was not a particle of anything with which to kindle a fire, unless we had used our wagon timber for that purpose, had we not sought the shelter of this friendly grove. We soon, resolved upon at least one week's rest in this place, and arrangements were made accordingly. During the week we feasted upon the most excellent wild meat, and spent most of our time in hunting and fishing.

Excepting the fear we constantly entertained concerning the Indians of the neighborhood, we spent the week here very pleasantly. One morning three large, fierce–looking Apaches came into camp at an early hour. They put on all possible pretensions of friendship; but from the first their movements were suspicious. They for a time surveyed narrowly our wagon and teams, and, so far as allowed to do so, our articles of food, clothing, guns, etc. Suspecting their intentions we bade them be off, upon which they reluctantly left our retreat. That night the dogs kept up a barking nearly the whole night, and at seasons of the night would run to their masters, and then a short distance into the wood, as if to warn us of the nearness of danger. We put out our fires, and each man, with his arms, kept vigilant guard. There is no doubt that by this means our lives were preserved. Tracts of a large number of Indians were seen near the camp next morning; and on going out we found that twenty head of stock had been driven away, some of which belonged to the teams. By this several of our teams were so reduced that we found extreme difficulty in getting along. Some of our wagons and baggage were left at a short distance from this in consequence of what we here lost. We traced the animals some distance, until we found the trail leading into the wild, difficult mountain fastnesses, where it was dangerous and useless to follow.

We were soon gathered up, and enroute again for "Ta Bac," another Mexican settlement, of which we had learned as presenting inducements for a short recruiting halt.

We found ourselves again traveling through a rich pasturage country, abounding with the most enchanting, charming scenery that had greeted us since we had left the "Big Bend." We came into "Ta Bac" with better spirits, and more vigorous teams, than was allowed us during the last few hundred miles.

At this place one of our number became the unwilling subject of a most remarkable and dampening transaction. Mrs. M., of "grape dumpling" notoriety, while bearing her two hundred and forty of avoirdupois about the camp at rather a too rapid rate, suddenly came in sight of a well that had been dug years before by the Mexican settlers.

While guiding her steps so as to shun this hugelooking hole, suddenly she felt old earth giving way beneath her. It proved that a well of more ancient date than the one she was seeking to shun had been dug directly in her way, but had accumulated a fine covering of grass during the lapse of years. The members of the camp, who were lazily whiling away the hours on the down hill–side of the well's mouth, were soon apprised of the fact that some momentous cause had interfered with nature's laws, and opened some new and hitherto unseen fountains in her bosom. With the sudden disappearance of Mrs. M., there came a large current of clear cold water flowing through the camp, greatly dampening our joys, and starting us upon the alert to inquire into the cause of this strange phenomenon. Mrs. M. we soon found safely lodged in the old well, but perfectly secure, as the water, on the principle that two bodies cannot occupy the same space at the same time, had leaped out as Mrs. M.'s mammoth proportions had suddenly laid an imperative possessory injunction upon the entire dimensions of the "hole in the ground."

We found, after leaving Ta Bac, the road uneven; the rains had set in; the nights were cold; and evidences of the constant nearness and evil designs of savage tribes were manifested every few miles that we passed over. Several once rich, but now evacuated, Mexican towns were passed, from which the rightful owners of the soil had been driven by the Apaches. At "Santa Cruz" we found a Mexican settlement of about one hundred inhabitants, friendly, and rejoiced to see us come among them, as they were living constantly in fear of the implacable Apaches, whose depredations were frequent and of most daring and outrageous character. Almost every day bands of these miscreant wretches were in sight upon the surrounding hills waiting favorable opportunities for the perpetration of deeds of plunder and death. They would at times appear near to the Mexican herdsmen, and tauntingly command them "to herd and take care of those cattle for the Apaches." We found the country rich and desirable, but for its being infested by these desperadoes. We learned, both firom the Mexicans and the conduct of the Indians themselves, that one American placed them under more dread and fear than a score of Mexicans. If along this road we were furnished with a fair representation, these Mexicans are an imbecile, frail, cowardly, and fast declining race. By the friendliness and generosity of the settlers at this point, we made a fine recruit while tarrying there. For a while we entertained the project of remaining for a year. Probably, had it not been for the prowling savages, whose thieving, murdering banditti infest field and woodland, we might have entered into negotiations with the Mexicans to this effect; but we were now en route for the Eureka of the Pacific Slope, and we thought we had no time to waste between us and the realization of our golden dreams. Every inducement that fear and generosity could invent, and that was in the power of these Mexicans to control, was, however, presented and urged in favor of our taking up a residence among them. But we had no certainty that our small number, though of the race most their dread, would be sufficient to warrant us in the successful cultivation of the rich and improved soil that was proffered us. Nothing but a constant guard of the most vigilant kind could promise any safety to fie]ds of grain, or herds of cattle.

We next, and at about eighty miles from Santa Cruz, came to Tukjon, another larger town than Santa Cruz, and more pleasantly, as well as more securely situated. Here again the same propositions were renewed as had been plied so vehemently at the last stopping–place. Such were the advantages that our hosts held out for the raising of a crop of grain, and fattening our cattle, that some of our party immnediately resolved upon at least one year's stay. The whole train halted here one month. During that time, those of our party who could not be prevailed upon to proceed, had arrangements made and operations commenced for a year of agricultural and farming employment.

At the end of one month the family of Wilders, Kellys, and ourselves, started. We urged on amid multiplying difficulties for several days. Our provisions had been but poorly replenished at the last place, as the whole of their crops had been destroyed by their one common and relentless foe, during the year. With all their generosity, it was out of their power to aid us as much as they would have done. Frequently after this, for several nights, we were waked to arm ourselves against the approaching Apaches, who hung in front and rear of our camp for nights and days.

Wearied, heart–sick, and nearly destitute, we arrived at the Pimo Village, on or about the 16th of February, 1851. Here we found a settlement of Indians, who were in open hostility to the Apaches, and by whose skill and disciplined strength they were kept from pushing their depredations further in that direction. But so long had open and active hostilities been kept up, that they were short of provisions and in nearly a destitute situation. They had been wont to turn their attention and energies considerably to farming, but during the last two years, their habits in this respect had been greatly interfered with. We found the ninety miles that divides Tukjon from Pimole to be the most dismal, desolate, and unfruitful of all the regions over which our way had led us as yet. We could find nothing that could, to a sound judgment, furnish matter of contention, such as had been raging between the rival claimants of its blighted peaks and crags.

Poor and desolate as were the war–hunted Pimoles, and unpromising as seemed every project surveyed by our anxious eyes for relief, and a supply of our almost drained stores of provisions, yet it was soon apparent to our family, that if we would proceed further we must venture the journey alone. Soon, and after a brief consultation, a full resolution was reached by the Wilders and Kellys to remain, and stake their existence upon traffic with the Pimoles, or upon a sufficient tarrying to produce for themselves; until from government or friends, they might be supplied with sufficient to reach Fort Yuma.

To Mr. Oatman this resolution brought a trial of a darker hue than any that had cast its shadows upon him as yet. He believed that starvation, or the hand of the treacherous savage, would soon bring them to an awful fate if they tarried; and with much reluctance he resolved to proceed, with no attendants or companions save his exposed and depressed family.

CHAPTER II

Mr. and Mrs. Oatman in Perplexity–Interview with Dr. Lecount Advises them to proceed–They start alone–Teams begin to fail–The Roads are bad–The Country rough and mountainous–Compelled to carry the Baggage up the Hills by Hand–Overtaken by Dr. Lecount on his way to Fort Yuma–He promises them Assistance from the Fort–The next Night the Horses of Dr. Lecount are stolen by the Apaches–He posts a Card, warning Mr. Oatman of Danger, and starts on Foot for the Fort–Reach the Gila River–Camp on the Island late at Night–Their dreary Situation, and the Conversation of the Children–The Morning of the 29th of March–Their Struggle to ascend the Hill on the 29th–Reach the Summit about Sunset–The Despondence and Presentiments of Mr. Oatman–Nineteen Apaches approach them Profess Friendliness–The Massacre–Lorenzo left for Dead, but is preserved–The Capture of Olive and Mary Ann.

Thi reader should here be apprised that, as the entire narrative that follows has an almost exclusive reference to those members of the family who alone survive to tell this sad tale of their sufferings and privations, it has been thought the most appropriate that it be given in the first person.

Lorenzo D. Oatman has given to the author the following facts, reaching on to the moment when he was made senseless, and in that condition left by the Apache murderers.

" We were left to the severe alternative of starting with a meagre supply, which any considerable delay would exhaust ere we could reach a place of re–supply, or to stay among the apparently friendly Indians, who also were but poorly supplied at best to furnish us; and of whose real intentions it was impossible to form any reliable conclusion. The statement that I have since seen in the 'Ladies' Repository,' made by a traveling correspondent who was at Pimole village at the time of writing, concerning the needlessness and absence of all plausible reason for the course resolved upon by my father, is incorrect. There were reasons for the tarrying of the Wilders and Kellys that had no pertinence when considered in connection with the peculiarities of the condition of my father's family. The judgment of those who remained, approved of the course elected by my father.

" One of the many circumstances that conspired to spread a gloom over the way that was before us, was the jaded condition of our team, which by this time consisted of two yoke of cows and one yoke of oxen. My parents were in distress and perplexity for some time to determine the true course dictated by prudence, and their responsibility in the premises. One hundred and ninety miles of desert and mountain, each alike barren and verdureless, save now and then a diminutive gorge (water–coursed and grassfringed, that miles apart led down from the high mountain ranges across the dreary road) strethednec out between us and the next settlement or habitation of man. We felt, deeply felt, the hazardous character of our undertaking; and for a time lingered in painful suspense over the proposed adventure. We felt and feared that a road stretching to such a distance, through an uninhabited and wild region, might be infested with marauding bands of the Indians who were known to roam over the mountains that were piled up to the north of us; who, though they might be persuaded or intimidated to spare us the fate of falling by their savage hands, yet might plunder us of all we had as means for life's subsistence. While in this dreadfull suspense, one Dr. Lecount, attended by a Mexican guide, came into the Pimole village. He was on his return from a tour that had been pushed westward, almost to the Pacific Ocean. As soon as we learned of his presence among us, father sought and obtained an interview with him. And it was upon information gained from him, that the decision to proceed was finally made.

"He had passed the whole distance to Fort Yuma, and returned, all within a few months,. unharmed; and stated that he had not witnessed indications of even the neighborhood of Indians. Accordingly, on the 11th of March, finding provisions becoming scarce among the Pimroles, and our own rapidly wasting, unattended, in a country and upon a road where the residence, or even the trace of one of our own nation would be sought in vain, save that of the hurrying traveler who was upon some official mission, or, as in the case of Dr. Lecount, some scientific pursuit requiring dispatch, we resumed our travel. Our teams were reduced; we were disappointed in being abandoned by our fellow–travelers, and wearied, almost to exhaustion, by the long and fatiguing march that had conducted us to this point. We were lengthening out a toilsome journey for an object and destination quite foreign to the one that had pushed us upon the wild scheme at first. And this solitary commencement on our travel upon a devious way, dismal as it was in every aspect, seemed the only alternative that gave any promise of an extrication fiom the dark and frowning perils and sufferings that were every day threatening about us, and with every step of advance into the increasing wildness pressing more and more heavily upon us."

Let the imagination of the reader awake and dwell upon the probable feelings of those fond parents at this trying juncture of circumstances; and when it shall have drawn upon the resources that familiarity with the heart's deepest anguish may furnish, it will fail to paint them with any of that poignant accuracy that will bring him into stern sympathy with their condition.

Attended by a family, a family which, in the event of their being overtaken by any of the catastrophes that reason and prudence bade them beware of on the route, must be helpless; if they did not, even by their presence and peculiar exposure, give point and power to the sense and presence of danger; a family entirely dependent upon them for that daily bread of which they were liable to be left destitute at any moment; far from human abodes, and with the possibility that, beyond the reach of relief, they might be set upon by the grini, ghastly demon of famine, or be made the victims of the blood–thirstiness and slow tortures of those human devils who, with savage ferocity, lurk for prey, when least their presence is anticipated; the faint prospect at best there was for accomplishing all that must be performed ere they could count upon safety; these, all these, and a thousand kindred considerations, crowded upon those lonely hours of travel, and furnished attendant reflections that burned through the whole being of these parents with the intensity of desperation. O! how many noble hearts have been turned out upon these dismal, death–marked by–ways, that have as yet formed she only land connection between the Atlantic and Pacific slopes, to bleed, and moan, and sigh, for weeks, and even months, suspended in painful uncertainty, between life and death at every moment. Apprehensions for their own safety, or the safety of dependent ones, like ghosts infernal, haunting them at every step. Fear, fear worse than death, if possible, lest sickness, famine, or the sudden onslaught of mnerciless savages, that infest the mountain fastnesses, and prowl and skulk through the innumerable hiding–places furnished by the wide sage–fields and chapparel, might intercept a journey, the first stages of which glowed with the glitter and charm of novelty, and beamed with the light of hope, but was now persisted in, through unforeseen and deepening gloom, as a last and severe alternative of selfpreservation, oppressed their hearts.

Monuments! monuments, blood–written, of these uncounted miseries, that will survive the longest lived of those most recently escaped, are inscribed upon the bleached and bleaching bones of our common humanity and nationality; are written upon the rude graves of our countrymen and kin, that strew these highways of death; written upon the moldering timbers of decaying vehicles of transport; written in blood that now beats and pulsates in the veins of solitaly and scathed survivors, as well as in the stain of kindred blood that still preserves its tale–telling, unbleached hue, upon scattered grass–plots, and Sahara sand mounds; written upon favored retreats, sought at the close of a dusty day's toil for nourishment, but suddenly turned into one of the unattended, unchronicled deathbeds, already and before fiequenting these highways of carnage and wrecks; written, ah! too sadly, deeply engraven upon the tablet of memories that keep alive the scenes of butcheries and captive–making that have rent and mangled whole households, and are now preserved to embitter the whole gloom–clad afterpart of the miraculously preserved survivors.

If there be an instance of one family having experienced trials that with peculiar pungency may suggest a train of reflection like the above, that family is the one presented to the reader's notice in these pages. Seven of them have fallen under the extreme of the dark picture; two only live to tell herein the tale of their own narrow escape, and the agonies which marked the process by which it came.

"For six days," says one of these, "our course was due southwest, at a slow and patience–trying rate. We were pressing through many difficulties, with which our minds were so occupied that they could neither gather nor retain any distinct impression of the country over which this first week of our solitary travel bore us. While thus, on the seventh day from Pimole, we were struggling and battling with the tide of opposition that, with the increasing force of multiplying embarrassments and drawbacks, was setting in against us, our teams failing and sometimes in the most difficult and dangerous places utterly refusing to proceed, we were overtaken by Dr. Lecount, who with his Mexican guide was on his way back to Fort Ynma. The doctor saw our condition, and his large, generous heart poured upon us a flood of sympathy, which, with the words of good cheer he addressed us, was the only relief it was in his power to administer Father sent by him, and at his own suggestion, to the fort for immediate assistance. This message the doctor promised should be conveyed to the fort, (we were about ninety miles distant from it at the time,) with all possible dispatch, also kindly assuring us that all within his power should be done to procure us help at once. We were all transiently elated with the prospect thus suddenly opening upon us of a relief from this source, and especially as we were confident that Dr. Lecount would be prompted to every office and work in our behalf, that he might command at the fort, where he was well and favorably known. But soon a dark cloud threw its shadow upon all these hopes, and again our wonted troubles rolled upon us with an augmented force Our minds became anxious, and our limbs were jaded. The roads had been made bad, at places almost impassable, by recent rains, and for the first time the strength and courage of my parents gave signs of exhaustion. It seemed, and indeed was thus spoken of among us, that the dark wing of some terrible calamity was spread over us, and casting the shadows of evil ominously and thickly upon our path. The only method by which we could make the ascent of the frequent high hills that hedged our way, was by unloading the wagon and carrying the contents piece by piece to the top; and even then we were often compelled to aid a team of four cows and two oxen to lift the empty wagon. It was well for us, perhaps, that there was not added to the burden of these long and weary hours, a knowledge, if the mishap that had befallen the messenger gone on before. About sunset of the day after Dr. Lecount left us, he camped about thirty miles ahead of us, turned his horses into a small valley hemmed in by high mountains, and with his guide slept until about daybreak. Just as the day was breaking and preparations were being made to gather up for a ride to the fort that day, twelve Indians suddenly emerged from behind a bluff hill near by and entered the camp. Dr. Lecount, taken by surprise by the presence of these unexpected visitants, seized his arms, and with his guide kept a close eye upon their movements, which he soon discovered wore a very suspicious appearance. One of the Indians would draw the doctor into a conversation, which they held in the Mexican tongue; during which others of the band would with an air of carelessness edge about, encircling the doctor and his guide, until in a few moments, despite their friendly professions, their treacherous intentions were plainly read. At the suggestion of his bold, intrepid, and experienced guide, they both sprang to one side, the guide presenting to the Indians his knife, and the doctor his pistol. The Indians then put on the attitude of fight, but feared to strike. They still continued their efforts to beguile the doctor into carelessness, by introducing questions and topics of conversation, but they could not manage to cover with this thin gauze the murder of their hearts. Soon the avenging ferocity of the Mexican began to burn, lie violcntly sprang into the air, rushed toward them brandishing his knife, and beckoning to the doctor to come on; he was about in the act of plunging his knife into the leader of the band, but was restrained by the coolness and prudence of Doctor Lecount. Manuel (the guide) was perfectly enraged at their insolence, and would again and again spring, tiger–like toward them, crying at the top of his voice, "terrily, terrily!" The Indians soon made off. On going into the valley for their animals they soon found that the twelve Indians had enacted the above scene in the camp, merely as a ruse to engage their attention, while another party of the same rascal band were driving their mules and horse beyond their reach. They found evidences that this had been done within the last hour. The doctor returned to camp, packed his saddle and packages in a convenient, secluded place near by, and gave orders to his guide to proceed immediately to the fort, himself resolving to await his return. Soon after Manuel had left, however, he bethought him of the Oatman family, of their imminent peril, and of the pledge he had put himself under to them, to secure them the earliest possible assistance; and he now had become painfully apprised of reasons for the most prompt and punctual fufillment of that pledge. He immediately prepared, and at a short distance toward us posted upon a tree near the road a card, warning us of the nearness of the Apaches, and relating therein in brief what had befallen himself at their hands; reassuring us also of his determined diligence to secure us protection, and declaring his purpose, contrary to a resolution he had formed on dismissing his guide, to proceed immediately to the fort, there in person to plead our case and necessities. This card we missed, though it was afterward found by those whom we had left at Pimole Village. What " might have been," could our eyes have fallen upon that small piece of paper, though it is now useless to conjecture, cannot but recur to the mind. It might have preserved fond parents, endeared brothers and sisters, to gladden and cheer a now embittered and bereft existence. But the card, and the saddle and packages of the doctor, we saw not until weeks after, as the sequel will show, though we spent a night at the same camp where the scenes had been enacted.

Toward evening of the eighteenth day of March, we reached the Gila River, at a point over eighty miles firom Pimole, and about the same distance from Fort Yuma.

We descended to the ford from a high, bluff hill, and found it leading across at a point where the river armed, leaving a small island sand–bar in the middle of the stream. We frequently found places on our road upon which the sun shines not, and for hours together the road led through a region as wild and rough as the imagination ever painted any portion of our earth. It was impossible, save for a few steps at a time, to see at a distance in any direction; and although we were yet inspirited at seasons with the report of Dr. Lecount, upon which we had started, yet we could not blind our eyes or senses to the possibilities that might lurk unseen and near, and to the advantages over us that the nature of the country about us would furnish the evil–designing foe of the white race, whose habitations we knew were locked up somewhere within these huge, irregular mountain ranges. Much less could we be indifferent to the probable inability of our teams to bear us over the distance still separating us from the place and stay of our hope. We attempted to cross the Gila about sunset; the stream was rapid, and swollen to an unusual width and depth. After struggling with danger and every possible hinderance until long after dark, we reached the sand island in the middle of the stream. Here our teams mired, our wagon dragged heavily, and we found it impossible to proceed.

"After reaching the center and driest portion of the island, with the wagon mired in the rear of us, we proceeded to detach the teams, and as best we could made preparations to spend the night. Well do I remember the forlorn countenance and dejected and jaded appearance of my father as he started to wade the lesser branch of the river ahead of us to gather material for a fire. At a late hour of that cold, clear,.wind–swept night, a camp–fire was struck, and our shivering group encircled it to await the preparation of our stinted allowance. At times the wind, which was blowing furiously most of the night, would lift the slight surges of the Gila quite to our camp–fire."

Let the mind of the reader pause and ponder upon the situation of that forlorn family at this time. Still unattended and unbefriended; without a white person or his habitation within the wide range of nearly a hundred miles; the Gila, a branch of which separated them from either shore, keeping up a ceaseless, mournful murmuriing through the entire night; the wild wind, as it swept unheeding by, sighing among the distant trees and rolling along the forest of mountain peaks, kept up a perpetual moan solemn as a funeral dirge. The imagination can but faintly picture the feelings of those fond parents upon whom hung such a fearful responsibility as was presented to their minds and thoughts by the gathering of this little loved family group about them.

"A large part of the night was spent by the children (for sleep we could not) in conversation upon our trying situation; the dangers, though unseen, that might be impending over our heads; of the past, the present, and the cloud–wrapt future; of the perils of our undertaking, which were but little realized under the light of novelty and hope that inspired our first setting out– an undertaking well–intentioned but now shaping itself so rudely and unseemly.

"We were compelled frequently to shift our position, as the fickle wind would change the point at which the light surges of the Gila would attack our camp–fire, in the center of that little island of about two hundred square feet, upon which we had of necessity halted for the night. While our parents were in conversation a little apart, which, too, they were conducting in a subdued tone for purposes of concealment, the curiosity of the elder children, restless and inquisitive, was employed in guessing at the probable import of their councils. We talked, with the artlessness and eagerness of our unrealizing age, of the dangers possibly near us, of the advantage that our situation gave to the savages, who were our only dread; and each in his or her turn would speak, as we shiveringly gathered around that little, threatened, sickly camp–fire, of his or her intentions in case of the appearance of the foe. Each had to give a map of the course to be pursued if the cruel Apaches should set upon us, and no two agreed; one saying, 'I shall run;' another,'I will fight and die fighting;' and still another,'I will take the gun or a club and keep them off;' and last, Miss Olive says, 'Well, there is one thing; I shall not be taken by these miserable brutes. I will fight as long as I can, and if I see that I am about to be taken, I will kill myself. I do not care to die, but it would be worse than death to me to be taken a captive among them.'"

How apprehensive, how timid, how frail a thing is the human mind, especially when yet untutored, and uninured to the severe allotments that are in this state incident to lengthened years. Experience alone can test the wisdom of the resolutions with which we arm ourselves for anticipated trials, or our ability to carry them out. How little it knows of its power or skill to triumph in the hour of sudden and trying emergency, only as the reality itself shall test and call it forth. Olive lives to–day to dictate a narrative of five gloomy years of captivity, that followed upon a totally different issue of an event that during that night, as a possibility merely, was the matter of vows and resolutions, but which in its reality mocked and taunted the plans and purposes that had been formed for its control.

"The longed–for twilight at length sent its earliest stray beams along the distant peaks, stole in upon our sand–bar camp, and gradually lifted the darkness from our dreary situation. As the curtain of that burdensome night departed, it seemed to bear with it those deep and awful shades that had rested upon our minds during its stay, and which we now began to feel had taken their gloomiest hue from the literal darkness and solitude that has a strange power to nurse a morbid apprehension. "Before us, and separating the shore from us, was a part of the river yet to be forded. At an early hour the teams were brought from the valley–neck of land, where they had found scant pasturage for the night, and attached to the wagon. We soon made the opposite bank. Before us was quite a steep declivity of some two hundred feet, by the way of the road. We had proceeded but a short distance when our galled and disarranged teams refused to go. We were again compelled to unload, and with our own hands and strength to bear the last parcel to the top of the hill. After this we found it next to impossible to compel the teams to drag the empty wagon to the summit.

"After reaching the other bank we camped, and remained through the heat of the day intending to travel the next night by moonlight. About two hours and a half before sunset we started, and just before the sun sank behind the western hills we had made the ascent of the hill and about one mile advance. Here we halted to reload the remainder of our baggage.

"The entire ascent was not indeed made until we reached this point, and to it some of our baggage had been conveyed by hand. I now plainly saw a sad, foreboding change in my father's manner and feelings. Hitherto, amid the most fatiguing labor and giant difficulties, he had seemed generally armed for the occasion with a hopeful countenance and cheerful spirit and manner, the very sight of which had a power to dispel our childish fears and spread contentment and resignation upon our little group. While ascending this hill I saw, too plainly saw, (being familiar, young as I was, with my father's aptness to express, by the tone of his action and manner, his mental state,) as did my mother also, that a change had come over him. Disheartening and soul–crushing apprehensions were written upon his manner, as if preying upon his mind in all the mercilessness of a conquering despair. There seemed to be a dark picture hung up before him, upon which the eye of his thought rested with a monomaniac intensity; and written thereon he seemed to behold a sad afterpart for himself, as if some terrible event had loomed suddenly upon the field of his mental vision, and though unprophesied and unheralded by any palpable notice, yet gradually wrapping its folds about him, and coming in, as it were, to fill his cup of anguish to the brim. Surely,

"'Coming events cast their shadows before them.
Who hath companioned a visit from the horn or ivory gate?
Who hath propounded the law that renders calamities gregarious?
Pressing down with yet more woe the heavy laden mourner;
Yea, a palpable notice warneth of an instant danger;
For the soul hath its feelers, cobwebs upon the wings of the wind,
That catch events, in their approach, with sure and sad pre sentiment.'

"Whether my father had read that notice left for our warning by Dr. Lecount, and had from prudence concealed it, with the impression it may have made upon his own mind, from us, to prevent the torment of fear it would have enkindled; or whether a campfire might have been discerned by him in the distance the night before, warning of the nearness of the savage Apaches; or whether by spirit law or the appointment of Providence the gloom of his waiting doom had been sent on before to set his mind in readiness for the breaking storm, are questions that have been indulged and involuntarily urged by his fond, bereaved children; but no answer to which has broke upon their ear from mountain, from dale, or from spirit–land. For one hour the night before my father had wept bitterly, while in the wagon thinking himself concealed from his family, but of which I was ignorant until it was told me by my eldest sister during the day. My mother was cain, cool, and collected; patient to endure, and diligent to do, that she might administer to the comfort of the rest of us. Of the real throbbings of the affectionate and indulgent heart of that beloved mother, her children must ever remain ignorant. But of her noble bearing under these trying circumstances angels might speak; and her children, who survive to cherish her name with an ardent, though sorrowing affection, may be pardoned for not keeping silence. True to the instincts that had ever governed her in all trying situations, and true to the dictates of a noble and courageous heart, she wisely attributed these shadows (the wing of which flitted over her own sky as well) to the harassings and exhaustion of the hour; she called them the accustomed creations of an overtasked mind, and then, with cheerful heart and ready hand, plied herself to all and any labors that might hie us upon our way. At one time, during the severest part of the toil and efforts of that day to make the summit of that hill, my father suddenly sank down upon a stone near the wagon, and exclaimed,'Mother, mother, in the name of God, I know that something dreadful is about to happen!' In reply, our dear mother had no expressions but those of calm, patient trust, and a vigorous, resolute purpose.

"'O, O Mother? bless'd sharer of our joys and woes,
E'en in the darkest hours of earthly ill,
Untarnish'd yet thy fond affection glow'd,
When sorrow rent the heart, when feverish pain
Wrung the hot drops of anguish from the brow;
To soothe the soul, to cool the burning brain,
O who so welcome and so prompt as thou?'

"We found ourselves now upon the summit, which proved to be the east edge of a long table–land, stretching upon a level, a long distance westward, and lying between two deep gorges, one on the right, the other on the left; the former coursed by the Gila River. We had hastily taken our refreshment, consisting of a few parcels of dry bread, and some beansoup, preparatory to a night's travel. This purpose of night travel had been made out of mercy to our famished teams, so weak that it was with difficulty they could be driven during the extreme sultry heat of the day. Besides this, the moon was nearly in full, giving us light nearly the entire night; the nights were cool, and better for travel to man and beast, and the shortness of our provisions made it imperative that we should make the most of our time."

Up, upon an elevated, narrow table–land, formed principally of lime rock, look now at this family; the scattered rough stones about them forming their seats, upon which they sit them down in haste to receive the frugal meal to strengthen them for the night's travel. From two years old and upward, that group of children, unconscious of danger, but dreading the lone, long hours of the night's journey before them. To the south of them, a wild, uninhabited, and uninhabitable region, made up of a succession of tablelands, varying in size and in height, with rough, verdureless sides, and separated by deep gorges and dark canons, without any vegetation save an occasional scrub–tree standing out from the general sterility. Around them, not a green spot to charm, to cheer, to enliven the tame, tasteless desolation and barrenness; at the foot of the bold elevation, that gives them a wider view than was granted while winding the difficult defiles of the crooked road left behind them, murmurs on the ceaseless Gila, upon which they gaze, over a bold precipice at the right. To the east and north, mountain ranges rising skyward until they seem to lean against the firmament. But within all the extended field swept by their curious, anxious vision, no smoking chimney of a friendly habitation appears to temper the sense of loneliness, or apprise them of the accessibleness of friendly sympathy or aid. Before them, a dusty, stony road points to the scene of anticipated hardships, and the land of their destination. The sun had scarcely concealed his burning face behind the western hills, ere the full–orbed moon peers from the craggy mountain chain in the rear, as if to mock at the sun weltering in his fading gore, and proffering the reign of her chastened, mellow light for the whole dreaded night.

"Though the sun had hid its glittering, dazzling face from us behind a tall peak in the distance, yet its rays lingered upon the summits that stretched away between us and the moon, and daylight was full upon us. Our hasty meal had been served. My father, sad, and seemingly spell–bound with his own struggling emotions, was a little on one side, as if oblivious of all immediately about him, and was about in the act of lifting some of the baggage to the wagon, that had as yet remained unloaded since the ascent of the hill, when, casting my eyes down the hill by the way we had come, I saw several Indians slowly and leisurely approaching us in the road. I was greatly alarmed, and for a moment dared not to speak. At the time, my father's back was turned. I spoke to him, at the same time pointing to the Indians. What I saw in my father's countenance excited in me a great fear, and took a deeper hold upon my feelings of the danger we were in, than the sight of the Indians. They were now approaching near us. The blood rushed to my father's face. For a moment his face would burn and flash as it crimsoned with the tide from within; then a death–like paleness would spread over his countenance, as if his whole frame was suddenly stiffened with horror. I saw too plainly the effort that it cost him to attempt a concealment of his emotions. He succeeded, however, in controlling the jerking of his muscles and his mental agitations, so as to tell us, in mild and composed accents,'not to fear; the Indians would not harm us.' He had always been led to believe that the Indians could be so treated as to avoid difficulty with them. He had been among them much in the Western states, and so often tried his theory of leniency with success that he often censured the whites for their severity toward them; and was disposed to attribute injury received from them to the unwise and cruel treatment of them by the whites. It had long been his pride and boast that he could manage the Indians so that it would do to trust them. Often had he thrown himself wholly in their power, while traveling and doing business in Iowa, and that, too, in times of excitement and hostility, relying upon his coolness, self–possession, and urbanity toward them to tamne and disarm their ferocity. As yet, his theory had worked no injury to himself, though often practiced against the remonstrances of friends. But what might serve for the treatment of the Iowa Indians, might need modification for these fierce Apaches. Besides, his wonted coolness and fearlessness seemed, as the Indians approached, to have forsaken him; and I have never been able to account for the conduct of my father at this time, only by reducing to reality the seemings of the past few days or hours, to wit, that a dark doom had been written out or read to him before.

"After the Indians approached, he became collected, and kindly motioned them to sit down; spoke to them in Spanish, to which they replied. They immediately sat down upon the stones about us, and still conversing with father in Spanish, made the most vehement professions of friendship. They asked for tobacco and a pipe, that they might smoke in token of their sincerity and of their friendly feelings toward us. This my father immediately prepared, took a whiff himself, then passed it around, even to the last. But amid all this, the appearance and conduct of father was strange. The discerning and interested eye of his agitated family could too plainly discover the uncontrollable, unspoken mental convulsions that would steal the march upon the forced appearances of composure that his better judgment, as well as yearnings for his family, dictated for the occasion. His movements were a reflecting glass, in which we could as plainly read some dire catastrophe was breeding for us, as well as in the flashes and glances that flew from face to face of our savage–looking visitants.

"After smoking, these Indians asked for something to eat. Father told them of our destitute condition, and that he could not feed them without robbing his family; that unless we could soon reach a place of new supplies we must suffer. To all this they seemed to yield only a reluctant hearing. They became

THE MASSACRE

earnest and rather imperative, and every plea that we made to them of our distress, but increased their wild and furious clamors. Father reluctantly took some bread from the wagon and gave it to them, saying that it was robbery, and perhaps starvation to his family. As soon as this was devoured they asked for more, meanwhile surveying us narrowly, and prying and looking into every part of the wagon. They were told that we could spare them no more. They immediately packed themselves into a secret council a little on one side, which they conducted in the Apache language, wholly unintelligible to us. We were totally in the dark as to their designs, save that their appearance and actions wore the threatening of some hellish deed. We were now about ready to start. Father had again returned to complete the reloading of the remainder of the articles; mother was in the wagon arranging them; Olive, with my older sister, was standing upon the opposite side of the wagon; Mary Ann, a little girl about seven years old, sat upon a stone holding to a rope attached to the horns of the foremost team; the rest of the children were on the opposite side of the wagon from the Indians. My eyes were turned away from the Indians.

Though each of the family was engaged in repairing the wagon, none were without manifestations of fear. For some time every movement of the Indians was closely watched by us. I well remember, however, that after a few moments my own fears were partially quieted, and from their appearance I judged it was so with the rest.

In a subdued tone frequent expressions were made concerning the Indians, and their possible intentions; but we were guarded and cautious, lest they might understand our real dread and be emboldened to violence. Several minutes did they thus remain a few feet from us, occasionally turning an eye upon us, and constantly keeping up a low earnest babbling among themselves. At times they gaged eagerly in various directions, especially down the road by which we had come, as if struggling to discern the approach of some object or person either dreaded or expected by them.

"Suddenly, as a clap of thunder from a clear sky, a defeaning yell broke upon us, the Indians jumping into the air, and uttering the most frightful shrieks, and at the same time springing toward us flourishing their war–clubs, which had hitherto been concealed under their wolf–skins. I was struck upon the top and back of my head, came to my knees, when with another blow, I was struck blind and senseless." One of their number seized and jerked Olive one side, ere they had dealt the first blow.

"As soon," continues Olive, "as they had taken me one side, and while one of the Indians was leading me off, I saw them strike Lorenzo, and almost at the same instant my father also. I was so bewildered and taken by surprise by the suddenness of their movements, and their deafening yells, that it was some little time before I could realize the horrors of my situation. When I turned around, opened my eyes, and collected my thoughts, I saw my father, my own dear father! struggling, bleeding, and moaning in the most pitiful manner. Lorenzo was lying with his face in the dust, the top of his head covered with blood, and his ears and mouth bleeding profusely. I looked around and saw my poor mother, with her youngest child clasped in her arms, and both of them still, as if the work of death had already been completed; a little distance on the opposite side of the wagon, stood little Mary Ann, with her face covered with her hands, sobbing aloud, and a hugelooking Indian standing over her; the rest were motionless, save a younger brother and my father, all upon the ground dead or dying. At this sight a thrill of icy coldness passed over me; I thought I had been struck; my thoughts began to reel and became irregular and confused; I fainted and sank to the earth, and for a while, I know not how long, I was insensible.

"When I recovered my thoughts I could hardly realize where I was, though I remembered to have considered myself as having also been struck to the earth, and thought I was probably dying. I knew that all, or nearly all of the family had been murdered; thus bewildered, confused, half conscious and and half insensible, I remained a short time, I know not how long, when suddenly I seemed awakened to the dreadful realities around me. My little sister was standing by my side, sobbing and crying, saying:'Mother, O mother! Olive, mother and father are killed, with all our poor brothers and sisters.' I could no longer look upon the scene. Occasionally a low, piteous moan would come from some one of the family as in a dying state. I distinguished the groans of my poor mother, and sprang wildly toward her, but was held back by the merciless savage holding–me in his cruel grasp, and lifting a club over my head, threatening me in the most taunting, barbarous manner. I longed to have him put an end to my life. 'O,' thought I, 'must I know that my poor parents have been killed by these savages and I remain alive!' I asked them to kill me, pleaded with them to take my life, but all my pleas and prayers only excited to laughter and taunts the two wretches to whose charge we had been committed.

"After these cruel brutes had consummated their work of slaughter, which they did in a few moments, they then commenced to plunder our wagon, and the persons of the family whom they had killed. They broke open the boxes with stones and clubs, plundering them of such of their contents as they could make serviceable to themselves. They took off the wagon wheels, or a part of them, tore the wagon covering off from its frame, unyoked the teams and detached them from the wagons, and commenced to pack the little food, with many articles of their plunder, as if preparatory to start on a long journey. Coming to a feather bed, they seized it, tore it open, scattering its contents to the winds, manifesting meanwhile much wonder and surprise, as if in doubt what certain articles of furniture, and conveniences for the journey we had with us, could be intended for. Such of these as they selected, with the little food we had with us that they could conveniently pack, they tied up in bundles, and started down the hill by the way they had come, driving us on before them. We descended the hill, not knowing their intentions concerning us, but under the expectation that they would probably take our lives by slow torture. After we had descended the hill and crossed the river, and traveled about one half of a mile by a dim trail leading through a dark, rough, and narrow defile in the hills, we came to an open place where there had been an Indian camp before, and halted. The Indians took off their packs, struck a fire, and began in their own way to make preparations for a meal. They boiled some of the beans just from our wagon, mixed some flour with water, and baked it in the ashes. They offered us some food, but in the most insulting and taunting manner, continually making merry over every indication of grief in us, and with which our hearts were ready to break. We could not eat. After the meal, and about an hour's rest, they began to repack and make preparations to proceed.

CHAPTER III

Lorenzo Oatman–Conscious of most of the Scenes of the Massacre–The next Day he finds himself at the Foot of a rocky Declivity, over which he had fallen–Makes an Effort to walk–Starts for Pimole HIis Feelings and Sufferings–Is attacked by Wolves–Then by two Indians, who are about to shoot him down–Their subsequent Kindness–They go on to the Place of Massacre–He meets the Wilders and Kellys–They take him back to Pimole–In about one Month gets well, and starts for Fort Yuma–Visits the Place of Massacre–His Feelings–Burial of the Dead–Reflections–The two Girls–Their Thoughts of Home and Friends–Conduct of their Captors–Disposition of the Stock–Cruelty to the Girls to hurry them on–Girls resolve not to proceed–Meet eleven Indians, who seek to kill Olive–Reasons for–Apaches defend her–Their Habits of Fear for their own Safety–Their Reception at the Apache Village One Year–The Mohaves–Their second coming among the Apaches–Conversation of Olive and Mary–Purchased by the Mohaves Avowed Reasons–Their Price–Danger during the Debate.

In this chapter we ask the reader to trace with us the narrow and miraculous escape of Lorenzo Oatman, after being left for dead by the Apaches. He was the first to receive the death–dealing blow of the perpetra tors of that horrid deed by which most of the family were taken from him. The last mention we made of him left him, under the effects of that blow, weltering in his blood. He shall tell his own story of the dreadful after–part. It has in it a candor, a freedom from the tinselings so often borrowed from a morbid imagination, and thrown about artificial romance, that commends it to the reader, especially to the juvenile reader. It exhibits a presence of mind, courage, and resoluteness that, as an example, may serve as a light to cheer and inspirit that boy whose eye is now tracing this record, when he shall find himself stumbling amid mishaps and pitfalls in the future, and when seasons of darkness, like the deep, deep midnight, shall close upon his path:

"I soon must have recovered my consciousness after I had been struck down, for I heard distinctly the repeated yells of those fiendish Apaches. And these I heard mingling in the most terrible confusion with the shrieks and cries of my dear parents, brothers, and sisters, calling, in the most pitiful, heart–rending tones, for' Help, help! In the name of God, cannot any one help us?'

"To this day the loud wail sent up by our dear mother from that rough death–bed still rings in my ears. I heard the scream, shrill, and sharp, and long, of these defenseless, unoffending brothers and sisters, distinguishing the younger from the older as well as I could have done by their natural voice; and these constantly blending with the brutal, coarse laugh, and the wild, raving whooping of their murderers. Well do I remember coming to myself, with sensations as of waking from a long sleep, but which soon gave place to the dreadful reality; at which time all would be silent for a moment, and then the silence broken by the low, subdued, but unintelligible gibberings of the Indians, intermingled with an occasional low, faint moan from some one of the family, as if in the last agonies of death. I could not move. I thought of trying to get up, but found I could not command a muscle or a nerve. I heard their preparations for leaving, and distinctly remenmber to have thought, at the time, that my heart had ceased to beat, and that I was about giving my last breath. I heard the sighs and moans of my sisters, heard them speak, knew the voice of Olive, but could not tell whether one or more was preserved with her.

"While lying in this state, two of the wretches came up to me, rolling me over with their feet; they examined and rifled my pockets, took off my shoes and hat in a hurried manner; then laid hold of my feet and roughly dragged me a short distance, and then seemed to leave me for dead. During all this, except for a moment at a time, occasionally, I was perfectly coscious, but could not see. I thought each moment would be my last. I tried to move again and again, but was under the belief that life had gone from my body and limbs, and that a few more breathings would shut up my senses. There seemed a light spot directly over my head, which was gradually growing smaller, dwindling to a point. During this time I was conscious of emotions and thoughts peculiar and singular, aside from their relation to the horrors about me. At one time (and it seemed hours) I was ranging through undefined, open space, with paintings and pictures of all imaginable sizes and shapes hung about me, as if at an immense distance, and suspended upon walls of ether. At another, strange and discordant sounds would grate on my ear, so unlike any that my ear ever caught, that it would be useless endeavoring to give a description of them. Then these would gradually die away, and there rolled upon my ear such strains of sweet music as completely ravished all my thoughts, and I was perfectly happy. And in all this I could not define myself; I knew not who I was, save that I knew, or supposed I knew, I had come from some far–off region, only a faint remembrance of which was borne along with me. But to attempt to depict all of what seemed a strange, actual experience, and that I now know to have been crowded into a few hours, would only excite ridicule; though there was something so fascinating and absorbing to my engaged mind, that I frequently long to reproduce its unearthly music and sights.

"After being left by the Indians, the thoughts I had, traces of which are still in my memory, were of opening my eyes, knowing perfectly my situation, and thinking still that each breath would be the last. The full moon was shining upon rock, and hill, and shrub about me; a more lovely evening indeed I never witnessed. I made an effort to turn my eye in search of the place where I supposed my kindred were cold in death, but could not stir. I felt the blood upon my mouth, and found it still flowing from my ears and nose. All was still as the grave. Of the fate of the rest of the family I could not now determine accurately to myself, but supposed all of them, except two of the girls, either dead or in my situation. But no sound, no voice broke the stillness of these few minutes of consciousness; though upon them there rested the weight of an anguish, the torture and horror of which pen cannot report. I had a clear knowledge that two or more of my sisters were taken away alive. Olive I saw them snatch one side ere they commenced the general slaughter, and I had a faint consciousness of having heard the voice and sighs of little Mary Ann, after all else was hushed, save the hurrying to and fro of the Indians, while at their work of plunder.

"The next period, the recollection of which conveys any distinct impression to my mind at this distance of time, was of again coming to myself blind, but thinking my eyes were some way tied from without. As I rubbed them, and removed the clotted blood from my eyelids, I gathered strength to open them. The sun, seemingly from mid–heaven, was looking me full in the face. My head was beating, and at times reeling under the grasp of a most torturing pain. I looked at my worn and tattered clothes, and they were besmeared with blood. I felt my head and found my scalp torn across the top. I found I had strength to turn my head, and it surpprised me. I made an effort to get up, and succeeded in rising to my hands and knees; but then my strength gave way. I saw myself at the foot of a steep, rugged declivity of rocks, and all about me new. On looking up upon the rocks I discovered traces of blood marking the way by which I had reached my present situation from the brow above me. At seasons there would be a return of partial aberration, and derangement of my intellect. Against these I sought to brace myself, and study the where and wherefore of my awful situation. And I wish to record my gratitude to God for enabling me then and there to collect my thoughts, and retain my sanity.

"I soon determined in my mind that I had either fallen, or been hurled down to my present position, from the place where I was first struck down. At first I concluded I had fallen myself, as I remembered to have made several efforts to get upon my hands and knees, but was baffled each time, and that during this I saw myself near a precipice of rocks, like that brow of the steep near me now, and that I plainly recognized as the same place, and now sixty feet or more above me. My consciousness now fully returned, and with it a painful appreciation of the dreadful tragedies of which my reaching my present situation had formed a part. I dwelt upon what had overtaken my family–kin, and though I had no certain mode of determining, yet I concluded it must have been the day before. Especially would my heart beat toward my fond parents, and dwell upon their tragical and awful end: I thought of the weary weeks and months by which they had, at the dint of every possible exertion, borne us to this point; ot the comparatively short distance that would have placed them beyond anxiety; of the bloody, horrid night that had closed in upon the troublous day of their lives.

"And then my thoughts would wander after those dear sisters; and scarcely could I retain steadiness of mind when I saw them, in thought, led away I knew not where, to undergo every ill and hardship, to suffer a thousand deaths at the hands of their heathen captors. I thought at times (being, I have no doubt, partially delirious) that my brain was loose, and was keeping up a constant rattling in my head, and accordingly I pressed my head tightly between my hands, that if possible I might retain it to gather a resolution for my own escape. When did so much crowd into so small a space or reflection before? Friends, that were, now re–presented themselves; but from them, now, my most earnest imploriings for help brought out no hand of relief; and as I viewed them, surrounded with the pleasures and joys of their safe home–retreats, the contrast only plunged me deeper in despair. My old playmates now danced before me again, those with whom I had caroled away the hours so merrily, and whom I had bidden the laughing, merry 'adieu,' only pitying them that they were denied the elysium of a romantic trip over the Plains. The scenes of sighs, and tears, and regrets that shrouded the hour of our departure firom kindred and friends, and the weeping appeals they plied so earnestly to persuade us to desist from an undertaking so freighted with hazard, now rolled upon me to lacerate and torture these moments of suffocating gaspings for breath.

"Then my own condition would come up, with new views of the unbroken gloom and despair that walled it in on every side, more impenetrable to the first ray of hope than the granite bulwarks about me to the light of the sun.

"A boy of fourteen years, with the mangled remains of my own parents lying near by, my scalp torn open, my person covered with blood, alone, friendless, in a wild, mountain, dismal, wilderness region, exposed to the ravenous beasts, and more, to the ferocity of more than brutal savages and humanshaped demons! I had no strength to walk, my spirits crushed, my ambition paralyzed, my body mangled. At times I despaired, and prayed for death; again I revived, and prayed God for help. Sometimes, while lying flat on my back, my hands pressing my torn and blood–clothed head, with the hot sun pouring a full tide of its unwelcome heat upon me, the very air a hot breath in my face, I gathered hope that I might yet look upon the white face again, and that I might live to rehearse the sad present in years to come. And thus bright flashes of hope and dark gloom–clouds would chase each other over the sky of my spirit, as if playing with my abandonment and unmitigated distress. 'And O,' thought I, 'those sisters, shall I see them again? must they close their eyes among those ferocious man–animals?' I grew sick and faint, dizziness shook my brain, and my senses fled. I again awoke from the delirium, partly standing, and making a desperate effort. I felt the thrill of a strong resolution. 'I will get up,' said I, 'and will walk, or if not I will spend the last remnant of my shattered strength to crawl out of this place.' I started, and slowly moved toward the rocks above me. I crept, snaillike, up the rock–stepped side of the table–land above me. As I drew near the top, having crawled almost fifty feet, I came in sight of the wagon wreck; then the scenes which had been wrought about it came back with horror, and nearly unloosed my hold upon the rocks. I could not look upon those faces and forms, yet they were within a few feet. The boxes, opened and broken, with numerous articles, were in sight. I could not trust my feelings to go further; 'I have misery enough, why should I add fuel to the fire now already consuming me!'

"I turned away, and began to crawl toward the east, round the biow of the hill. After carefully, and with much pain, struggling all the while against faintness, crawling some distance, I found myself at the slope leading down

Lorenzo Returning to the Place of Massacre

to the Ford of the Gila, where I plainly saw the wagon track we had made, as I supposed, the day before. The hot sun affected me painfully; its burning rays kindled my fever, already oppressive, to the boiling point. I felt a giant determination urging me on. Frequently my weariness and faiutness would bring me to the griolnd several times in a few moments. Then I would crawl aside, (as I did immediately after crossing the river,) drag myself under some mountain shrub for escape from the sun, bathe my fevered head in its friendly shade, and lay me to rest. Faint as I was firom loss of blood, and a raging inward thirst, these, even, were less afflicting than the meditations and reflections that, unbidden, would at times steal upon my mind, and lash it to a perfect phlrenzy with agonizing remembrances. The groans of those parents, brothers, and sisters, haunted me with the grim, fiend–like faces of their murderers, and the flourishing of their war–clubs; the convulsive throbs of little Mary Ann would fill my mind with sensations as dreary as if my traveling had been among the tombs.

"'O my God!' said I,'am I alive? My poor father and mother, where are they? And are my sisters alive? or ate they suffering death by burning? Shall I see them again?'

"Thus I cogitated, and wept, and sighed, until sleep kindly shut out the harrowing thoughts. I must have slept for three hours, for when I woke the sun was behind the western hills. I felt refreshed, though suffering still from thirst. The road crosses the bend in the river twice; to avoid this, I made my way over the bluff spur that turns the road and river to the.north. I succeeded after much effort in sustaining myself upon my feet, with a cane. I walked slowly on, and gained strength and courage that inspired within some hope of my escape. I traveled on, only taking rest two or three times during that evening and whole night. I made in all about fifteen miles by the next day–break. About eleven o'clock of the next day I came to a pool of standing water; I was nearly exhausted when I reached it and lay me down by it, and drank freely, though the water was warm and muddy. I had no sooner slaked my thirst than I fell asleep and slept for some time. I awoke partially delirious, believing that my brain was trying to jump out of my head, while my hands were pressed to my head to keep it together, and prevent the exit of my excited brain. When I had proceeded about ten miles, which I had made by the middle of the afternoon, I suddenly became faint, my strength failed, and I fell to the ground. I was at the time upon a high table–land, sandy and barren. I marveled to know whether I might be dying; I was soon unconscious. Late in the afternoon I was awakened by some strange noise; I soon recollected my situation, and the noise, which I now found to be the barking of dogs or wolves, grew louder and approached nearer. In a few moments I was surrounded by an army of coyotes and gray wolves. I was lying in the sun, and was faint from the effects of its heat. I struggled to get to a small tree near by, but could not. They were now near enough for me to almost reach them, smelling, snuffing, and growling as if holding a meeting to see which shoilid be first to pllnge his sharp teeth in imy flesh, and first to gor ge his lank stomach upon my almost bloodless

Lorenzo Attacked by Coyotes and Wolves

carcass. I was excited with fear, and immediately sprang to my feet and raised a yell; and as I rose, struck the one nearest me with my hand. i–e started back, and the rest gave way a little. This was the first utterance I had made since the massacre. These unprincipled gormandizers, on seeing me get up and hurl a stone at them, ran off a short distance, then turned and faced me; when they set up one of the most hideous, doleful howlings that I ever heard from any source. As it rang out for several minutes upon the still evening air, and echoed from crag to crag, it sent the most awful sensations of dread and loneliness thrilling through my whole frame. 'A fit requiem for the dead,' thought I. I tried to scatter them, but they seemed bent upon supplying their stomachs by dividing my body between them, and thus completing the work left unfinished by their brothers, the Apaches.

"I had come now to think enough of the chance for my life, to covet it as a boon worth preserving. But I had serious fears when I saw with what boldness and tenacity they kept upon my track, as I armed myself with a few rocks and pushed on. The excitement of this scene fully roused me, and developed physical strength that I had not been able before to command. The sun had now reached the horizon, and the first shades of lonely night lay upon the distant gorges and hill–sides. I kept myself supplied with rocks, occasionally hurling one at the more insolent of this second tribe of savages. They seemed determined, however, to force an acquaintance. At times they would set up one of their wild concerts, and grow furious as if newly enraged at my escape. Then they would huddle about, fairly besetting my steps. I was muilch frightened, but knew of only one course to take. After becoming weary and faint with hunger and thirst, some time after dark I feared I should faint, and before morning be dovoured by them. Late in the evening they called a halt, for a moment stood closely huddled in the road behind me, as if wondering what blood–clad ghost from some other sphere could be treading this unfriendly soil. They were soon away, to my glad surprise; and ere midnight the last echo of their wild yells had died upon the distant hills to the north. I traveled nearly all night. The cool night much relieved the pain in my head, but compelled me to keep up beyond my strength, to prevent suffering from cold. I have no remembrance of aught from about two to four o'clock of that night, until about nine of the next day, save the wild, troublous dreams that disturbed my sleep. I dreamed of Indians, of bloodshed, of my sisters, that they were being put to death by slow tortures, that I was with them, and my turn was coming soon. When I came to myself I had hardly strength to move a muscle; it was a long time before I could get up. I concluded I must perish, and meditated seriously the eating of the flesh from my arm to satisfy my hunger and prevent starvation. I knew I had not sufficient of life to last to Pimole at this rate, and concluded it as well to lie there and die, as to put forth more of painful effort.

"In the midst of these musings, too dreadful and ftill of horror to be described, I roused and started. About noon I was passing through a dark cafion, nearly overhung with dripping rocks; here I slaked my thirst, and was about turning a short corner, when two red–shirted Pimoles, mounted upon fine American horses, came in sight. They straightened in their stirrups, drew their bows, with arrows pointed at me. I raised my hand to my head and beckoned to them, and speaking in Spanish, begged them not to shoot. Quick

Lorenzo Rescued by Friendly Indians

as thought, when I spoke they dropped their bows, and rode up to me. I soon recognized one of them as an Indian with whom I had been acquainted at Pimole Village. They eyed me closely for a few minutes, when my acquaintance discovering through my disfigured features who it was, that I was one of the family that had gone on a little before, dismounted, laid hold of me, and embraced me with every expression of pity and condolence that could throb in an American heart. Taking me by the hand they asked me what could have happened. I told them as well as I could, and of the fate of the rest of the family. They took me onc sidc under a tree, and laid me upon their blankets. They then took from their saddle a piece of their ash–baked bread, and a gourd of water. I ate the piece of bread, and have often thought of the mercy it was they had no more, for I might have easily killed myself by eating too much; my cravings were uncontrollable. They hung up the gourd of water in reach, and charged me to remain until they might return, promising to carry me to Pimole. After sleeping a short time I awoke, and became fearful to trust myself with these Pimoles. They had gone on to the scene of the massacre; it was near night; I adjusted their blankets and laid them one side, and commenced the night's travel refreshed, and not a little cheered. But I soon found my body racked with more pain, and oppressed with more weariness than ever. I kept up all night, most of thie time traveling. It was the loneliest, most horrorstruck night of nmy life. Glad was I to mark the first streaks of the fourth morning. Never did twilight shine so bright, or seem empowered to chase so much of darkness away.

"Cheered for a few moments, I hastened my steps, staggering as I went; I found that I was compelled to rest oftener than usual, I plainly saw I could not hold out much longer. My head was becoming inflamed within and without, and in places on my scalp was putrid. About mnid–forenoon, after frequent attempts to proceed, I crawled under a shrub and was soon asleep, I slept two or three hours undisturbed. 'O my God!' were the words with which I woke, 'could I get something to eat, and some one to dress my wounds, I might yet live.' I had now a desire to sleep continually. I resisted this with all the power I had. While thus musing I cast my eyes down upon a long winding valley through which the road wandered, and plainly saw moving objects; I was sure they were Indians, and at the thought my heart sank within me. I meditated killing myself. For one hour I kept my aching eyes upon the strange appearance, when, all at once, as they rose upon a slight hill, I plainly recognized two white covered wagons. O what a moment was that. Hope, joy, confidence, now for the first time seemed to mount my soul, and hold glad empire over all my pains, doubts, and fears. In the excitement I lost my consciousness, and waked not until disturbed by some noise near me. I opened my eyes, and two covered wagons were halting close to me, and Robert was approaching nme. I knew him, but my own appearance was so haggard and unnatural, it was some time before he detected who that 'strangelooking boy, covered with blood, hatless and shoeless, could be, his visage scarred, and he pale as a ghost fresh firom Pandemonium.' After looking for some time, slowly and cautiously approachling,, he broke out: 'My God, Lorenzo! in the name of heaven, what, Lorenzo, has happened?' I felt my heart strangely swell in my bosom, and I could scarcely believe my sight. 'Can it be?' I thought, 'can it be that this is a familiar white face?' I could not speak; my heart could only pour out its emotions in the streaming tears that flowed most freely over my face. When I recovered myself sufficiently, I began to speak of the fate of the rest of the family. They could not speak, some of them; those tender–hearted women wvept most bitterly, and sobbed aloud, begging me to desist, and hide the rest of the truth from them.

"They immediately chose the course of prudence, and resolved not to venture with so small a company, where we had met such a doom. Mr. Wilder prepared me some bread and milk, which, without any necessity for a sharpening process, my appetite, for some reason, relished very well. They traveled a few miles on the back track that night, and camped. I received every attention and kindness that a true sympathy could minister. We camped where a gurgling spring sent the clear cold water to the surface; and here I refreshed myself with draughts of the purest of beverages, cleansed my wounds, and bathed my aching head and bruised body in one of nature's own baths. The next day we were safe at Pimole ere night came on. When the Indians learned what had happened, they, with much vehemence, charged it upon the Yumas; but for this we made allowance, as a deadly hostility burned between these tribes. Mr. Kelly and Mr. Wilder resolved upon proceeding immediately to the place of massacre, and burying the dead.

"Accordingly, early the next day, with two Mexicans and several Pimoles, they started. They returned after an absence of three days, and reported that they could find but little more than the bones of six persons, and that they were able to find and distinguish the bodies of all but those of Olive and Mary Ann. If they had found the bodies of my sisters the news would have been less dreadful to me than the tidings that they had been carried off by the Indians. But my suspicions were now confirmed, and I could only see them as the victims of a barbarous captivity. During their absence, and for some time after, I was severely and dangerously ill, but with the kind attention and nursing rendered me I began after a week to revive. We were now only waiting the coming that way of some persons who might be westward bound, to accompany them to California. When we had been there two weeks, six men came into Piminole, who, on learning of our situation, kindly consented to keep with us until we could reach Fort Yuma. The Kellys and Wilders had some time before abandoned their notion of a year's stay at Pimole. We were soon again upon that road, with every step of which I now had a painful familiarity. On the sixth day we reached that place, of all others the most deeply memorywritten. I have no power to describe, nor can tongue or pen proclaim the feelings that heaved my sorrowing heart as I reached the fatal spot. I could hear still the echo of those wild shrieks and hellish whoops, reverberating along the mountain cliffs! those groans, those awful groans, could it be my imagination, or did they yet live in pleading. echo among the numerous caverns on either hand? Every footfall startled me, and seemed to be an intruder upon the chambers of the dead!

"There were dark thoughts in my mind, and I felt that this was a charnel–house that had plundered our household of its bloom, its childhood, and its stay! I marked the precise spot where the work of death commenced. My eyes would then gaze anxiously and long upon the high, wild mountains, with their forests and peaks that now embosomed all of my blood that were still alive! I traced the footprints of their captors, and of those who had laid my parents beneath my feet. I sighed to wrap myself in their death–robe, and with them sleep my long, last sleep! But it was haunted ground, and to tarry there alive was more dreadful than the thought of sharing their repose. I hastened away. I pray God to save me in future from the dark thoughts that gloomed my mind on turning my back upon that spot; and the reader from experiencing kindred sor row. With the exception of about eighteen miles of desert, we had a comfortable week of travel to Fort Yuma. I still suffered much, at times was seriously worse, so that my life was despaired of; but more acute were my mental than my physical sufferings.

"At the Fort every possible kindness, with the best of medical skill, ministered to my comfort and hastened my recovery. To Dr. Hewitt I owe, and must forever owe, a debt of gratitude which I can never return. The sense of obligations I still cherish finds but a poor expression in words. He became a parent to me; and kindly extended his guardianship and unabating kindness, when the force was moved to San Diego, and then he took me to San Francisco, at a time when, but for his counsel and his affection ate oversight, I might have been turned out to wreck upon the cold world.

"Here we found that Doctor Lecount had done all in his power to get up and hasten a party of men to our relief; but he was prevented by the commander, a Mir. Heinsalman, who was guilty of an unexplailiable, if not an inexcusable delay–a delay that was an affliction to the doctor, and a calamity to us. He seemed deaf to every appeal for us in our distressed condition. His conduct, if we had been a pack of hungry wolves, could not have exhibited more total recklessness. The fict of our condition reached the Fort at almost as early an hour as it would if the animals of the doctor had been retained, and there were a number of humane men at the Fort who volunteered to rush to our relief; but no permission could be obtained from the commander. If he still lives, it is to know and remember, that by a prompt action at that time, according to the behests and impulse of a principle of 'humanity to man,' he would have averted our dreadful doom. No language can fathom such cruelty.–i.e. was placed there to protect the defenseless of his countrymen; and to suffer an almnost destitute family, struggling amid dangers and difficulties, to perish for want of relief that he knew he might have extended, rolls upon him a responsibility in the inhuman tragedy that followed his neglect, that will haunt him through eternity. There were men there who nobly stepped forward to as sime the danger and labor of the prayed–for relief, and around them clusters the light of gratitude, the incense of the good; but he who neglects the destitute, the hungry, the imperiled, proclaims his companionship with misanthropists, and hews his own road to a prejudged disgrace. After several days he reluctantly sent out two men, who hastened on toward Pimole until they came to the place of the massacre, and finding what had happened, and that the delay had been followed by such a brutal murder of the family for whose safety and rescue they had burned to encounter the perils of this desert way, sick at heart, and indignant at this cruel, let–alone policy, they returned to the Fort; though not until they had exhausted their scant supply of provisions in search of the girls, of whose captivity they had learned. May Heaven bless these benefactors, and pour softening influences upon their hard–hearted commander."

The mind instinctively pauses, and, suspended between wonder and horror, dwells with most intense interest upon a scene like the one presented above. Look at the faint pointings to the reality, yet the best that art can inscribe, furnished by the plate. Two timid girls, one scarcely fourteen, the other a delicate, sweet–spirited girl of not eight summers. Treimbling with fear, swaying and reeling under the wild storm of a catastrophe bursting upon them when they had been lulled into the belief that their danger–tlhronged path had been well–nigh passed, and the fury of which exceeded all that the most excited imagination could have painted, these two girls, eye–witnesses to a brutal, bloody affray which had smitten father, mother, brothers, and sisters, robbing them in an instant of friends and friendly protection, and cast themselves, they knew not where, upon the perpetrators of all this butchery, whose tender mercies they had only to expect would be cruelty itself. That brother, that oldest brother, weltering in his blood, perfectly conscious of all that was transpiring. The girls wishing that a kindred fate had ended their own sufferings, and preserved them by a horrible death from a more horrible afterpart, placing them beyond the reach of savage arm and ferocity. O what an hour was that! What a world of paralyzing agonies were pressed into that one short hour! It was an "ocean in a tear, a whirlwind in a sigl, an eternity in a moment." Unoffending, innocent, yet their very souls throbbing with woe they had never merited. See them but a little before, wearied with the present, but happy in the prospect of a fast approaching termination of their journey. A band of Indians, stalwart, stout, and fierce–looking, came into the camp, scantily clad, and what covering they had borrowed firom the wild beasts, as if to furnish an appropriate badge of their savage nature and design. They cover their weapons under their wolf–skins; they warily steal upon this unprotected family, and by deceiving pretenses of friendship blunt their apprehensions of danger, and make them oblivious of a gathering doom. They smoke the pacific pipe, and call themselves Pimoles who are on their way to Fort Yuma. Then secretly they concoct their hellish plot in their own tongue, with naught but an involuntary glance of their ser pent eyes to flash or indicate the infernality of their treacherous hearts. When every preparation is made by the family to proceed, no defense studied or thought necessary, then these hideous man–animals spring upon them with rough war–clubs and murder them in cold blood; and, as if to strew their hellish way with the greatest possible amount of anguish, they compel these two girls to witness all the barbarity that broke upoin the rest, and to read therein what horrors hung upon their own future living death. O what depths and deeds of darkness and crime are sometimes locked up in that heart where the harmonies of a passion–restraining principle and reason have never been waked up! How slender every foundation for any forecasting upon the character of its doings, when trying emergences are left an appeal to its untamed and unregulated propensities!

The work of plunder follows the work of slaughter. The dead bodies were thrown about in the rudest manner, and pockets searched, boxes broken and plundered, and soon as they are fully convinced that the work of spoils–taking is completed, and they discover no signs of remaining life (which they hunted for diligently) to awaken suspicions of detection, they prepare with live spoils, human and brute, to depart.

"Soon after," continues Olive, "we camped. A fire was struck by means of flints and wild cotton, which they carried for the purpose. The cattle were allowed to range upon the rock–feed, which abounded; and even with this unnatural provision, they were secure against being impelled by hunger far from camp, as? they scarcely had strength to move. Then came the solid dough, made of water and flour, baked stone–hard in the hot ashes, and then soaked in beansoup; then the smoking of pipes by some, while others lounged lazily about the camp, filled up the hour of our tarrying here. Food was offered me, but how could I eat to prolong a life I now loathed. I felt neither sensations of hunger nor a desire to live. Could I have done it, I should probably have ended my life during moments of half–delirious, crushing anguish, that some of the time rolled upon me with a force sufficient to divide soul from body. But I was narrowly watched by those worse than fiends, to whom every expression of my grief was occasion for merry–making. I dwelt upon these awful realities, yet, at times, such I could not think ,hemn to be, until my thoughts would become confused. Mangled as I knew they were, I longed to go back and take one look, one long, last, farewell took in the faces of my parents and those dear brothers. Could I but go back and press the hands of those dear ones though cold in death, I would then consent to go on! There was Lucy, about seventeen years of age, a dear girl of a sweet, mild spirit, never angry. She had been a mother to me when our parents were absent or sick. She had borne the peculiar burden falling upon the oldest of a family of children, with evenness of temper and womanly fortitude. 'Why,' my heart inquired, 'should she be thus cut off and I left?' Lorenzo I supposed dead, for I saw him fall to the ground by the first blow that was struck, and afterward saw them take from him hat and shoes, and drag him to the brink of the hill by the feet. Supposing they would dash him upon the rocks below, I turned away, unable to witness more! Royse, a playful, gleeful boy, full of health and happiness, stood a moment horror–struck as he witnessed the commencement of the carnage, being furthest from the Indians. As they came up to him, he gave one wild, piercing scream, and then sank to the earth under the club! I saw him when the death–struggle drew his little frame into convulsions, and then he seemed to swoon away; a low moan, a slight heaving of the bosom, and he quietly sank into the arms of death. Little C. A. had not as yet seen four summers; she was a cherub girl. She, with her little brother, twenty months younger, had been saved the torments of fear that had seized the rest of us from the time of the appearance of the Indians. They were too young to catch the flashes of fear that played upon the countenances of the elder children and their parents, and were happily trustful when our father, with forced composure, bade us not be afraid! The struggles of these two dear little ones were short. My mother screamed, I turned, I saw her with her youngest child clasped in her arms, and the blows of the war–club falling upon her and the child. I sprang toward her, uttered a shriek, and found myself joining her in calling most earnestly for help. But I had no sooner started toward her than I was seized and thrown back by my overseer. I turned around, found my head beginning to reel in dizziness, and fainting fell to the ground.

"The reader can perhaps imagine the nature of my thoughts while standing at that camp–fire, with my sister clinging to me in convulsive sobs and groans. From fear of the Indians, whose frowns and threats, mingled with hellish jests, were constantly glaring upon us, she struggled to repress and prevent any outburst of the grief that seemed to tear her little heart. And when her feelings became uncontrollable, she would hide her head in my arms, and most piteously sob aloud, but she was immediately hushed by the brandishing of a war–club over her head.

"While in this camp, awaiting the finished meal, and just after twilight, the full moon arose and looked in upon our rock–girt gorge with a majesty and sereneness that seemed to mock our changeful doom. Indeed a more beautiful moonrise I never saw. The sky was clear, the wind had hushed its roar, and laid by its fury; the larger and more brilliant of the starry throng stood ouit clear above, despite the superior light of thle moon, which lhad blutshed the lesser ones into obscurity. As that moon mounted the cloudless east, yet tinged withl the last stray beauties of twilight, and sent its first mild glories along, the surrounding peaks, the scene of illuminled heights, and dark, cavernous, shade–clad hill–sides and gorg,es, was grand, and to a mind

The Captives at the Indian Camp–fire

unfettered with woe would have lent the inspiration of song. I looked upon those goirges and vales, with their deeps of gloom, and then upon the moon–kissed ridges that formed boundaries of light to limit their shadows! I thought the former a fit exponent of my heart's realizations, and the whole an impressive illustration of the contrast between my present and the recent past. That moon, ordinarily so welcome, and that seemed supernaturally empowered to clothe the barren heights with a richer than nature's verdure robes, and so cheering to us only a few evenings previous while winding our way over that dusty road, had now suddenly put on a robe of sackcloth. All was still, save the chattering of our captors, and the sharp, irregular howling of the coyotes, who perform most of their odes in the night, and frequently made it hideous firom twilight to twilight again.

"O how much crowded into that short hour spent at the first camp after leaving the scene of death and sleeping previous! Ignorant of the purposes of our own preservation, we could only wait in breathless anxiety the movements of our merciless lords. I then began to meditate upon leaving those parents, brothers and sisters; I looked up and saw the uncovered bows strung over the wagon, the cloth of which had been torn off by the Indians. I knew that it designated the spot where horror and affection lingered. I meditated upon the past, the present, and the future. The moon, gradually ascending the sky, was fast breaking in upon the deep–shade spots that at her first rising had contended with ridges of light spread about them. That moon had witnessed the night before my childish but sincerest vow, that I would never be taken alive by Indian savages, and was now laughing at the frailty of the resolution and the abruptness with which the fears to which it pointed had become reality! That moon had smiled on many, very many hours spent in lands far away in childish glee, romps and sports prolonged, near the home–hearth and grass–plotted door–yard, long after the cool evening breezes had fanned away the sultry air of the day. The very intonations of the voices that had swelled and echoed in those uncaring hours of glee came back to me now, to rehearse in the ears of a present, insupportable sorrow, the music of past, but happier days. This hour, this moon–Iit Hour, was one most dear and exclusive to the gushing forth of the heart's unrestrained overflowings of happiness. Where are now those girls and boys? where now are those who gathered about me, and over whose suntanned but ruddy cheeks had stolen the unbidden tear at the hour of parting; or, with an artless simplicity, the heart's' good–by' was repeated o'er and o'er again? Is this moon now bearing the same uinmingled smile to them as when it looked upon our mutual evening promenadings? or has it put on the somber hues that seem to tinge its wonted brightness to me, heralding the color of our fate, and hinting of our sorrow? These, all these, and many more kindred reflections found way to, and strulg, the heart's saddest notes. And as memory and present consciousness told me of those days and evenings gone–gone never to be repeated–I became sick of life, and resolved upon stopping its currents with my own hands; and but for the yearning anxiety that bent over little MIlary Ann, I should have only waited the opportunity to have executed my desperate purpose. The strolls to school, arm–in–arm with the now remembered, but abandoned partners of the blissful past, on the summer morn; the windings and wanderings upon the distinctly remembered strawberry patches at sultry noon; the evening walks for the cows, when the setting sun and the coming on of cloudless, storiuless, cool evenings, clothed all nature with unwonted loveliness; together with the sad present, that fuirnished so unexpected and tormenting a contrast with all before, would rush again upon me, bringing the breath of dark, suicidal thoughts to fire up the jfrst hour of a camp amoty the flndians!" But these harrowing meditations are suddenly interrupted; cattle are placed in order for traveling; five of the Indians are put in charge of the girls, and welcome or unwelcome they must away they knew not where.

"We were started and kept upon a rapid pace for several hours. One of the Indians takles the lead, Mary Ann and myself follow, bareheaded and shloeless, the Indians having taken off our shoes and head covering. We were traveling at a rate, as we soon learned, much beyond our strength. Soon the light of the camp–fire was hid, and as my eye turned, full of tears, in search of the sleeping–place of my kindred, it could not be distinguished from the peaks and rocks about it. Every slackening of our pace and utterance of grief, however, was the signal for new threats, and the suspended war–club, with the fiendish 'Yokoa' in our ears, repressed all expression of sorrow, and pushed us on up steeper ascents and bolder hills with a quickened step. We must have traveled at the rate of four or five miles an hour. Our feet were soon lacerated, as in shadowed places we were unable to pick our way, and were frequently stumbling upon stones and rocks, which made them bleed freely. Little, Alary Ann soon became unable to proceed at the rate we had been keeping, and sank down after a few miles, saying she could not go. After threatening and beating her considerably, and finding this treatment as well as my entreaties useless, they threatened to dispatch and leave her, and showed by their movements and gestures that they had fully come to this determination. At this I knew not what to do; I only wished that if they should do this I might be left with her. She seemed to have become utterly fearless of death, and said she had rather die than live. These inhuman wretches sought by every possible rudeness and abuse to rouse her fears and compel her on; but all in vain. I resolved, in the event of her being left, to cling to her, and thus compel them to dispose of us as they had the remainder of the family, and leave us upon a neighboring hill. My fears wvere that I could not succeed in my desperate purpose, and I fully believed they would kill her, and probably compel me on with them. This fear induced me to use every possible plea that I could make known to them to preserve her life; besides, at every step a faint hope of release shone upon my heart; that hope had a power to comfort and keep me up. While thus halting, one of the stout Indians dislodged his pack, and putting it upon the shoulders of another Indian, rudely threw Mary Ann across his back, and with vengeance in his eye bounded on.

"Sometimes I meditated the desperate resolution to utterly refuse to proceed, but was held back alone by my yearning for that helpless sister. Again, I found my strength failing, and that unless a rest could be soon granted I must yield to faintness and weariness, and bide the consequences; thus I passed the dreadful hours up to midnight. The meanings and sobbings of Mary Ann had now ceased; not knowing but she was dead, I managed to look in her face, and found her eyes opening and shutting alternately, as if in an effort to wake, but still unable to sleep; I spoke to her but received no answer. We could not converse without exciting the fiendish rage of our enemies. Mary Ann seemed to have become utterly indifferent to all about her; and, wrapped in a dreamy reverie, relieved of all care of life or death, presenting the appearance of one who had simply the consciousness that some strange, unaccountable event had happened, and in its bewildering effects she was content to remain. Our way had been mostly over a succession of small bluff points of high mountain chains, these letting down to a rough winding valley, running principally northeast. These small rock hills that formed the bottom of the high cliffs on either side, were rough, with no perceptible trail. We halted for a few moments about the middle of the night; besides this we had no rest until about noon of the next day, when we came to an open place of a few acres of level, sandy soil, adorned with an occasional thrifty, beautiful tree, but high and seemingly impassable mountains hemming us in on every side. This appeared to be to our captors a familiar retreat. Almost exhausted, and suffering extremely, I dragged myself up to the place of halt, hoping that we had completed the travel of that day. We had tarried about two hours when the rest of the band, who had taken the stock in another direction, came up. They had with them two oxen and the horse. The rest of the stock, we afterward learned, had been killed and hung up to dry, awaiting the roving of this plundering band when another expedition should lead them that way. Here they immediately proceeded to kill the other two. This being done they sliced them up, and closely packed the parcels in equalized packages for their backs. They then broiled some of the meat on the fire, and prepared another meal of this and burned dough and bean soup. They offered us of their fare and we ate with a good appetite. Never did the tender, wellprepared veal steak at home relish better than the tough, stringy piece of meat about the size of the hand, given us by our captors, and which with burned dough and a little bean soup constituted our meal. We were very sleepy, but such was my pain and suffering I could not sleep. They endeavored now to compel Mary Ann again to go on foot; but this she could not do, and after beating her again, all of which she took without a murmur, one of them again took her upon his shoulder and we started. I had not gone far before I found it impossible to proceed on account of the soreness of my feet. They then gave me something very much of the substance of sole–leather which they tied upon the bottom of my feet. This was a relief, and though suffering much from thirst and the pain of over–exertion, I was enabled to keep up with the heavy–laden Indians. We halted in a snug, dark ravine about ten o'clock that night, and preparations were at once made for a night's stay. My present suffering had now made me almost callous as to the past, and never did rest seem so sweet as when I saw they were about to encamp.

"During the last six hours they had whipped Mary Ann into walking. We were now shown a soft place in the sand, and directed to it as the place of our rest; and with two of our own blankets thrown over us, and three savages encircling us, (for protection of course!) were soon, despite our physical sufferings, in a dreamy and troubled sleep. The most frightful scenes of butchery and suffering followed into every moment's slumber. We were not roused until a full twilight had shone in upon our beautiful little ravine retreat. The breakfast was served up, consisting of beef, burned dough, and beans, instead of beans, burned dough, and beef, as usual. The sun was now fairly upon us when, like cattle, we were driven forth to another day's travel. The roughest road (if road be a proper term) over which I ever passed, in all my captivity, was that day's route. Twice during the day, I gave up, and told Mary I must consent to be murdered and left, for proceed I would not. But this they were not inclined to allow. When I could not be driven, I was pushed and hauled along. Stubs, rocks, and gravel–strewn mountain sides hedged up and embittered the travel of the whole day. That day is among the few days of my dreary stay among the savages, marked by the most pain and suffering ever endured. I have since learned that they hurried for fear of the whites, emigrant trains of whom were not unfrequently passing that way. For protection they kept a close watch, having not less than three guards or sentinels stationed at a little distance from each camp we made during the entire night. I have since thought much upon the fear manifested by these reputed brave barbarians. They indeed seem to be borne down with the most tormenting fear for their personal safety at all times, at home, or roaming for plunder or hunt. And yet courage is made a virtue among them, while cowardice is the unpardonable sin. When compelled to meet death, they seem to muster a sullen obstinate defiance of their doom, that makes the most of a dreaded necessity, rather than seek a preparation to meet it with a submission which they often dissemble but never possess.

"About noon we were suddenly surprised by coming upon a band of Indians, eleven in number. They emerged from behind a rock point that set out into a low, dark ravine, through which we were passing, and every one of them was armed with bows and arrows. When they came up they were jabbering and gesturing in the most excited manner, with eyes fastened upon me. While some of them were earnestly conversing with members of our band, two of them stealthily crept around us, and one of them by his gestures and excited talk, plainly showed hostile intentions toward us, which our captors watched with a close eye. Suddenly one of them strung his bow, and let fly an arrow at me, which pierced my dress, doing me no harm.

Attempt to Shoot Olive and Mary Ann

"He was in the act, as also the other, of hurling the second, when two of our number sprang toward them with their clubs, while two others snatched us one side, placing themselves between us and the drawn bows. By this time a strong Apache had the Indian by a firm grasp, and compelled him to desist. It was with difficulty they could be shaken off, or their murderous purpose prevented. At one time there was likely to be a general fight with this band (as I afterward learned them to be) of land pirates.

"The reason, as I afterward came to know, of the conduct of this Indian, was that he had lost a brother in an affray with the whites upon this same Santa Fe' route, and he had sworn not to allow the first opportunity to escape without avenging his brother's blood by taking the life of an American. Had their number been larger a serious engagement would have taken place, and my life have probably been sacrificed to this fiend's revenge. During the skirmish of words that preceded and for some time followed this attempt upon my life, I felt but little anxiety, for there was little reason to hope but that we must both perish at the best, and to me it mattered little how soon. Friends we had none; succor, or sympathy, or help, we had no reason to think could follow us into this wild, unknown region; and the only question was Whether we should be murdered inch by inch, or find a sudden though savage termination to our dreadful condition, and sleep at once quietly beyond the reach or brutality of these fiends in death's embrace. Indeed death seemed the only release proffered from any source. If I had before known that the arrow would lodge in life's vitals, I doubt whether it would have awakened a nerve or moved a muscle.

"We traveled until about midnight, when our captors called a halt, and gave us to understand we might sleep for the remainder of the night. But, jaded as we were, and enduring as we were all manner of pain, these were not more in the way of sleep than the wild current of our anxious thoughts and meditations, which we found it impossible to arrest or to leave with the dead bodies of our dear kindred. There was scarcely a moment when the mind's consent could be gained for sleep. Well do I remember to have spent the larger proportion of that half of a night in gazing upon the stars, counting those directly over head, calling the names I had been taught to give to certain of the planets, pointing out to my sister the old dipper, and seeking to arrest and relieve her sadness by referring to the views we had taken of these from the old grass–clad door–yard in front of our humble cottage in Illinois. We spoke of the probability that these might now be the objects of attention and sight to eyes far away; to eyes familiar, the gleam of whose kindly radiance had so oft met ours, and with the strength of whose vision we had so delightfully tried our own in thus star–gazing. These scenes of a past yet unfinished childhood came rushing upon the mind, bidding it away over the distance that now separated them and their present occupants firom us, and to think mournfully of the still wider variance that separated their allotment from ours. Strange as it may appear, scenes and woes like those pressing upon us had a power to bind all sensitiveness about our fate. Indeed, indifference is the last retreat of desperation. The recklessness observed in the Indians, their habits of subsistence, and all their manner and bearing toward their captives, could lead them only to expect that by starvation or assassination they must soon become the victims of a brutal fate.

"On the third day we came suddenly in sight of a cluster of low, thatched huts, each having an opening near the ground leading into them."

It was soon visible from the flashing eyes and animated countenances of the Indians, that they were nearing some place of attraction, and to which anxious and interesting desire had been pointing. To two young girls, having traveled on foot two hundred miles in three days; with swollen feet and limbs, lame, exhausted, not yet four days remove from the loss of parents, brothers, and sisters, and torn from them, too, in the most brutal manner; away in the deeps of forests and mountains, upon the desolation of which the glad light or sound of civilization never yet broke; with no guides or protectors, rudely, inhumanly driven by untutored, untamed savages, the sight of the dwelling–places of man, however coarse or unseemly, was no very unwelcome scene. With all the dread possibilities, therefore, that might await them at any moment, nevertheless to get even into an Indian camp was home.

"We were soon ushered into camp, amid shouts and song, wild dancing, and the crudest, most irregular music that ever ranter sung, or delighted the ear of an unrestrained superstition. They lifted us on the top of a pile of brush and bark, then formed a circle about us of men, women, and children of all ages and sizes, some naked, some dressed inll blankets, some in skins, some

Indian Skulking to Hear the Conversation of the Girls

in bark. Music then commenced, which consisted of pounding upon stones with clubs and horn, and the drawing of a small string like a fiddle–bow across distended bark. They ran, and jumped, and danced in the wildest and most furious manner about us, but keeping a regular circle. Each, on coming to a certain point in the circle, marked by a removed piece of turf in the ground, would bend himself or herself nearly to the ground, uttering at the same time a most frightful yell, and making a violent gesticulation and stamping. Frequently on coming near us, as they would do in each evolution, they would spit in our face, throw dirt upon us, or slightly strike us with their hand, managing, by every possible means, to give us an early and thorough impression of their barbarity, cruelty, and obscenity. The little boys and girls, especially, would make the older ones merry by thus taunting us. It seemed during all this wild and disgusting performance, that their main ambition was to exhibit their superiority over us, and the low, earnest, intense hate they bore toward our race. And this they most effectually succeeded in accomplishing, together with a disgusting view of the obscenity, vulgarity, and grossness of their hearts, and the mean, despicable, revengeful dispositions that burn with hellish fury within their untamed bosoms.

"We soon saw that these bravadoes had made themselves great men at home. They had made themselves a name by the exploits of the past week. They had want only set upon a laboring family of nine persons, unprotected, and worn to fatigue by the toils of a long journey, without any mode of defense, and had inhumanly slaughtered seven of them, taken two inoffensive girls into a barbarous captivity, and drove them two hundred miles in three days without that mercy which civilization awards to the brute; taken a few sacks of smoked, soot–covered cow–meat, a few beans, a little clothing, and one horse! By their account, and we afterward ascertained that they have a mode of calculating distances with wonderful accuracy, we had come indeed over two hundred and fifty miles, inside of eighty hours.

"This may seem incredible to the reader, but the rate at which we were hurried on, the little rest that was granted, and subsequent knowledge gained of their traveling rate, confirms the assertion made by themselves as to the distance.

"We found the tribe to consist of about three hundred, living in all the extremes of filth and degradation that the most abandoned humanity ever fathomed. Little had the inexperience and totally different habits of life, from which these reflections are made, of the knowledge or judgment to imagine or picture the low grossness to which unrestrained, uneducated passions can sink the human heart and life. Their mode of dress, (but little dress they had!) was needlessly and shockingly indecent, when the material of which their scanty clothing consists would, by an industrious habit and hand, have clothed them to the dictates of comfort and modesty.

"They subsisted principally upon deer, quail, and rabbit, with an occasional mixture of roots from the ground. And even this dealt out with the most sparing and parsimonious hand, and in quantity only up to a stern necessity; and this, not because of poverty in the supply, but to feed and gratify a laziness that would not gather or hunt it.

"It was only when the insatiable and half–starved appetite of the members was satisfied, when unusual abundance chanced to come in, that their captives could be allowed a morsel; and then their chance was that of the dogs, with whom they might share the crumbs. Their meat was boiled with water in a 'Tusquin,' (clay kettle,) and this meat–mush or soup was the staple of food among them, and of this they were frequently short, and obliged to quiet themselves with meted out allowance; to their captives it was always thus meted out. At times game in the immediate vicinity was scarce, and their indolence would not let them go forth to the chase upon the mountains and in the valleys a little distance, where they acknowledged it plenty, only in cases of impending starvation. During the time of captivity among them, very frequently were whole days spent without a morsel, and then when the hunter returned with game, he was surrounded with crowds hungry as a pack of wolves to devour it, and the bits and leavings were tauntingly thrown to 'Onatas,' saying, 'You have been fed too well; we will teach you to live on little.' Besides all this, they were disbelievers in the propriety of treating female youth to meat, or of allowing it to become their article of subsistence; which, considering their main reliance as a tribe upon game, was equal to dooming their females to starvation. And this result of their theory became a mournful and constantly recurring fact. According to their physiology the female, especially the young female, should be allowed meat only when necessary to prevent starvation. Their own female children frequently died, and those alive, old and young, were sickly and dwarfish generally.

"Several times were their late captives brought near a horrid death ere they could be persuaded to so waive their superstitious notions as to give them a saving crumb.

"These Apaches were without any settled habits of industry. They tilled not. It was a marvel to see how little was required to keep them alive; yet they were capable of the greatest endurance when occasion taxed their strength. They ate worms, grasshoppers, reptiles, all flesh, and were, perhaps, living exhibitions of a certain theory by which the nature of the animal eaten leaves its imprint upon the man or human being who devours it. For whole days, when scarcely a morsel for another meal was in the camp, would those stout, robust, lazy lumps of a degraded humanity lounge in the sun or by the gurgling spring; at noon in the shade or own the shelves of the mountains surrounding, utterly reckless of their situation, or of the doom their idleness might bring upon the whole tribe. Their women were the laborers and principal burden–

bearers, and dturing all our captivity," says Olive, "it was our lot to serve under these enslaved women, with a severity more intolerable than that to which they were subjected by their merciless lords. They invented modes, and seemed to create necessities of labor, that they might gratify themselves by taxing us to the utmost, and even took unwarranted delight in whipping us on beyond our strength. And all their requests and exactions were couched in the mnost insulting and taunting language and manner, as it then seemed, and as they had the frankness soon to confess, to fiume their hate against the race to whom we belonged.

"Often under the frown and lash were we compelled to labor for whole days upon an allowance amply sufficient to starve a common dandy civilized idler, and those days of toil wrung out at the instance of children younger than ourselves, who were set as our task–masters. They knew nothing of cultivating the soil. After we had learned their language enouglh to talk with them, we ventured to speak to them of the way by which we had lived, of the tilling of the ground.

"They had soil that might have produced, but most of them had an abhlorrence of all that might be said of the superior blessings of industry and the American civilization. Yet there were those, especially among the females and the younger members of the tribe, who asked frequent questions, and with eagerness, of our mode of life. For some time after coming among them, Mary Ann was very ill. The fatigue, the cruelties of the journey, nearly cost her her life; yet in all her weakness, sickness, and pinings, they treated her with all the heartlessness of a dog. She would often say to me: 'Olive, I must starve unless I can get something more to eat;' yet it was only when she was utterly disabled that they would allow her a respite from some daily menial service. We have often taken the time which was given to gather roots for our lazy captors, togather and eat ourselves; and had it not been for supplies obtained by such means, we must have perished. But the physical sufferings of this state were light when compared with the fear and anguish of mind; the bitter fatc upon us, the dismal remembrances that harassed us, the knowledge of a bright past and a dark future by which we were cornpassed, these, all these belabored every waking moment, and crowded the wonted hours of sleep with terrible forebodings of a worse fate still ahead. Each day seemed to be allotted its own peculiar woes; some circumstance, some new event would arise, touehing and enkindling its own class of bitter emotions. We were compelled to heed every whimper and cry of their little urchins with promptness, and fully, under no less penalty than a severe beating,, and that in the most severe manner. These every–day usages and occurrences would awaken thorny reflections upon our changed and prison life. There was no beauty, no loveliness, no attractions in the country possessed by these unlovely creatures to make it pleasant, if there had been the blotting out of all the dreadful realities that had marked our way to it, or the absence of the cruelties that made our stay a living death. Often has my little sister come to me with a heart surcharged with grief, and the big tears standing in her eye, or perhaps sobbing most convulsively over the maltreatment and chastisement that had met her good intentions, for she ever tried to please them, and most piteously would she say: 'How long, O how long, dear Olive, must we stay here; can we never get away? do you not think they intend to kill us? O! they are so ugly and savage!' Sometimes I would tell her that I saw but little chance for escape; that we had better be good and ready for any fate, and try to wait in submission for our lot.

"She would dry her eyes, wipe the tears away, and not seldom have I known her to return with a look of pensive thoughtfulness, and that eye, bright and glistening with the light of a new–born thought, as she would say: 'I know what we can do; we can ask God. He can deliver us, or give us grace to bear our troubles.' It was our custom to go by ourselves and commit ourselves to God in faithful prayer every day; and this we would do after we laid our weary frames upon our sand bed to rest, if no other opportunity offered. This custom had been inculcated in us by a fond and devoted mother, and well now did we remember with what affection she assured us that we would find it a comfort and support to thus carry our trials and troubles to our heavenly Father in after years; though little did she realize the exceedingly bitter grief that would make these lessons of piety so sweet to our hearts. Too sadly did they prove true. Often were the times when we were sent some distance to bring water and wood for the comfort of lazy men, selected for the grateful observance of this only joyful employment that occupied any of those dark days.

"Seldom during our stay here were we cheered with any knowledge or circumstance that bid us hope for our escape. Hours were spent by us in talking of trying the experiment. Mary often would say: 'I can find the way out, and I can go the whole distance as quick as they.' Several times, after cruel treatment, or the passing of danger from starvation, have we made the resolution, and set the time for executing it, but were not bold enough to undertake it. Yet we were not without all or any hope. A word dropped by our captors concerning their occasional trips, made by small bands of them to some region of the whites, some knowledge we would accidentally gain of our latitude and locality, would animate our breasts with the hope of a future relief, breaking like a small ray of light from some distant luminous object upon the eye of our faith. But it was only when our minds dwelt upon the power of the Highest, on an overruling Providence, that we could feel that there was any possibility of an extrication from our uncheered prison life.

"After we had been among these Apaches several months, their conduct toward us somewhat changed. They became more lenient and merciful, especially to my sister. She always met their abuse with a mild, patient spirit and deportment, and with an intrepidity and fortitude beyond what might have been expected from her age. This spirit, which she always bore, I could plainly see was working its effect upon some of them; so that, especially on the part of those females connected in some way with the household of the chief, and who had the principal control of us, we could plainly see more forbearance, kindness, and interest exhibited toward their captives. This, slight as was the change, was a great relief to my mind, and comfort to Mary Ann. We had learned their language so as to hold converse with them quite understandingly, after a few months among them. They were much disposed at times to draw us into conversation; they asked our ages, inquired after our former place of living, and when we told them of the distance we had come to reach our home among them, they greatly marveled. They would gather about us frequently in large numbers, and ply their curious questions–with eagerness and seeming interest, asking how many of the white folks there were; how far the big ocean extended; and on being told of the two main oceans, they asked if the whites possessed the other big world on the east of the Atlantic; if there were any Indians there; particularly they would question us as to the number of the 'Americans,' (this term they obtained among the Mexicans, and it was the one by which they invariably designated our people.) When we told them of the number of the whites, and of their rapid increase, they were apparently incredulous, and some of them would become angry, and accuse us of lying, and wishing to make them believe a lie. They wanted to know how women were treated, and if a man was allowed more than one wife; inquired particularly how and by what means a subsistence was gained by us. In this latter question we could discern an interest that did not inspire any of their other queries. Bad as they are, they are very curious to know the secret of the success and increase of the whites. We tried to tell them of the knowledge the whites possessed, of the well–founded belief they had that the stars above us were peopled by human beings, and of the fact that the distance to these far–off worlds had been measured by the whites. They wished to know if any of us had been there; this they asked in a taunting manner, exhibiting in irony and sarcasm their incredulity as to the statement, over which they made much sport and ridicule. They said if the stars were inhabited, the people would drop out, and hence they knew that this was a lie. I found the months and years in which I had been kept in school, not altogether useless in answering their questions. I told them that the earth turned round every twenty–four hours, and also of its traveling about the sun every year. Upon this they said we were just like all the Americanos, big liars, and seemed to think that our parents had begun young with us to learn us so perfectly the art of falsehood so early. But still we could see, through all their accusations of falsehood, by their astonishment, and discussion, and arguments upon the matter of our conversation, they were not wholly unbelieving. They would tell.us, however, that an'evil spirit' reigned among the whites, and that he was leading them on to destruction. They seemed sincere in their belief that there were scarcely any of the whites that could be trusted, but that they had evil assistance, which made them great and powerful. As to any system of religion or morality, they seemed to be beneath it. But we found, though the daily tasks upon us were not abated, yet our condition was greatly mollified; and we had become objects of their growing curiosity, mere playthings, over which they could make merry.

"They are much given to humor and fun, but it generally descends to low obscenity and meanness. They had great contempt for one that would complain under torture or suffering, even though of their own tribe, and said a person that could not uncom plainingly endure suffering was not fit to live. They asked us if we wanted to get away, and tried by every stratagem to extort from us our feelings as to our captivity; but we were not long in learning that any expression of discontent was the signal for new toils, and tasks, and grievances. We made the res elution between us to avoid any expression of dis content, which, at times, it cost us no small effort to keep.

"We learned that this tribe was a detached parcel of the old and more numerous tribe bearing their name, and whose locality was in the regions of NewMexico. They had become in years gone, impatient of the restraint put upon them by the Catholic missioinaies, and had resolved upon emancipation from their control, and had accordingly sought a home in the wild fastnesses of these northern mountains. The old tribe had since given them the name of the 'Touto Apaches,' an appellation signifying their unruliness, as well as their roving and piratical habits. They said that the old tribe was much more wicked than themselves, and that they would be destroyed by the whites."

Beyond the manuscript touching the geography and appearance of the country where the scenes of this book were laid, and which was prepared for previous editions, there is considerable concerning the peculiar superstitions and crude beliefs of these Indians, as well as upon histories treasured up by them touching their tribes and individual members of them, which we believe would be read with interest, but scarcely a tithe of which can we give without swelling this book beyond all due bounds. Of these histories it is not to be supposed that more than mere scraps could have been gleaned by Olive, when we remember her age, and that all that is remembered is from mere verbal recital.

The Indians would congregate on evenings set apart, when one of their number, most in years and of prominent position, would entertain the company with a narration, frequently long and tedious, of the adventures of his youthful days. On one of these occasions an old Indian spoke as follows: "I am the son of an Indian who was chief of the Camanche tribe. I had heard often of the white people. I longed to see one. I was told by my father one day that I might, with some of the warriors of the tribe, go on a hunt to the north, and also that we would probably find some white people; if so, that we must kill them, and bring in their scalps with any white captive girls if we could find them. We had so many (counting his fingers up to three) bows and so many (forty–eight) arrows each.

"The most of my desire was to see and kill a white man, and take some captives. We traveled a very long way. We passed through several tribes of Indians. We found, according to the accounts of some Indians away to the north, that there were white people near them, but that we must not touch them; that they were friendly and traded with themselves; that some of their squaws were married to them; that they (the whites) came from the great Auhah (sea) to the setting sun. One day, about dark, we came in view of an object that we thought at first to be a bear. We soon found it was a man. We waited and skulked for some time to find out, if possible, whether it was a man, and how many of them there were. We stayed all night in this condition, and it was very cold. Just before fair day, we moved slowly round the place where we had seen the object. As we thought we had got past it and not espied anything, we concluded to go on, when we were suddenly met by a huge–lookiig thing with a covering (skin) such as we had never before seen. We were surprised and did not know what to do. It was partly behind a rock, and we were too much scared to draw our bows. After a word together, (there were four of us,) we concluded to run. So we started. We had not gone far when an Indian jumped out after us, threw an umsupieque (white blanket) from his head, and called to us to stop. We had never seen this umsupieque before. We were very much ashamed. We thought at first, and when we ran, that some of our friends had been killed and had come (or their ghosts) to meet us. The Indian, a Chimowanan, came up to us, and began to laugh at our bravery! We were much ashamed, but we could not help it now. We left the Indian, after making him promise that lie would not tell of us.

"When we had traveled one day, with no game or anything to eat, we came to a small house built of wood. We thought it the house of a white man. We skulked in the bushes, and thought we would watch it until they should come out, or, if away, come home. We waited one day and two nights, eating nothing but a few roots. We saw no one, so we set fire to the house and went on. We were more afraid of the Indians than the whites, for they had said they would kill us if we touched the whites. A few days after this we saw another house; we watched that a long time, then burned it, and started for home. This is all we did. When we came home our tribe turned out to see us, and hear of our war–hunt. We had but little to say.

"The next year, the Indian who had scared us with the white blanket, came among us. I saw him, and made him promise not to tell my father what a coward I had shown myself when I met him; but I soon found that all the tribe knew all about it. When the tribe were gathered together one day for a dance, they laughed at me and about me for my running from the Indian. I found that the Indian had told some of the tribe, and they had told my father.

My father joined with the rest in making fun of me for it. I blamed him, and felt mad enough to kill him. He found it out, so, just before we separated. he called them all together, and told them that he had displeased his son by what he had said of me, and now he wanted to make it all right. He said, just before he sat down, that if ever they should be attacked, he should feel that they were safe, that he knew his son and those who went north to kill white people would be safe, for they had shown themselves good at running. This maddened me more than ever, and up to this day I have not heard the last of my running from the Indian. I am now old, my head is nearly bald, the hairs that have fallen from my head have grown up to be some of these I now see about me. I shall soon go to yonder hill. I want you to burn my bow and arrow with my body, so that I can hunt up there."

"The'Toutos' had, however, for a long time occupied their present position, and almost the only tribe with whom they had any intercourse was the Mohaves, (Mo–ha–vays,) a tribe numbering about twelve hundred, and located three hundred miles to the northwest.

"There were many, however, who had come from other and different tribes. Some from the north, some from the south and southwest. Hence there was a marked distinction among their features and appearance. It seemed from what we could learn that this Touton tribe, or secession firagment, had from their villianous propensities fled to this hidingplace, and since their separation been joined by scattered members and stray families from other tribes, persons whom Touton bands had fallen in with during their depredating trips abroad, and who from community of feeling and life had thus amalgamated together.

"For a few years constant traffic had been kept up between the Mohaves and Toutons. The Mohaves made an expedition once a year, sometimes oftener, to the Apaches, in small companies, bringing with them vegetables, grain. and the various products of their soil, which they would exchange with the Apaches for fur, skins of animals, and all of the few articles that their different mode of life furnished. During the autumn of 1851, late in the season, quite a large company of Mohaves came among us on a trading expedition. But the whole transactions of one of these expeditions did not comprise the amount of wealth or business of one hour's ordinary shopping of a country girl. This was the first acquaintance we had with those superior Indians. During their stay we had some faint hints that it was meditated to sell us to the Mohaves in exchange for vegetables, which they no doubt regarded as more useful for immediate consumption than their captives. But still it was only a hint that had been given us, and the curiosity and anxiety it created soon vanished, and we sank again into the daily drudging routine of our dark prison life. Months rolled by, finding us early and late at our burden–bearing and torturing labors, plying hands and feet to heed the demands of our lazy lords, and the taunts and exactions of a swarm of heathen urchins, sometimes set over us. But since the coming of these Mohaves a new question had been presented, and a new source of anxious solicitude had been opened. Hours at a time were spent apart, dwelling upon and conversing about the possibilities and probabilities, with all the gravity of men in the council of state, of our being sold to another tribe, and what might be its effects upon us. At times it was considered as the possible means by which an utter and hopeless bondage might be sealed upon us for life. It was seen plainly that the love of traffic predominated among these barbarous hordes; that the lives of their captives would be but a small weight in the balance, if they interfered with their lust of war or conquest, if gain without toil might be gratified. It was feared that the deep–seated hostility which they bore to the white race, the contempt which they manifested to their captives, united with the fear (which their conduct had more than once exhibited) that they might be left without that constant, vigilant oversight that was so great a tax upon their indolence to maintain over them, that they might return to their own people and tell the tale of their sufferings and captivity, and thus bring down upon them the vengeance of the whites; that all these causes might induce them to sell their captives to the most inaccessible tribe, and thus consign them to a captivity upon which the light of hope or the prospect of escape could not shine."

On a little mound, a short distance from the clustered, smoking wigwams, constituting the Apache village, on a pleasant day, see these two captive girls, their root baskets laid aside, and side by side upon the ground, sitting down to a few moments' conversation. They talk of the year that has now nearly closed, the first of their captivity, the bitterness that had mingled in the cup of its allotment, of their dead, who had now slept one year of their last sleep, and with much concern they are now querying about what might be the intentions of the Mohaves in their daily expected comining again so soon among the Apaches.

Mary Ann says: "I believe they will sell us; I overheard one of the chiefs say something the other day in his wigwam, about our going among the Mohaves, and it was with some words about their expected return. I do not know, but from what I saw of them I think they know more, and live better than these miserable Apaches."

Olive. "But may be they put on the best side when here, they might treat us worse than the Apaches."

M.A. "O, that will be impossible without they kill us, and if we cannot escape, the sooner we die the better. I wish, Olive, you would agree to it, and we will start to–night and try to make our escape"

O. "But where shall we go? We know not the way we came, much of it was traveled in the night, besides this, these Indians have their trails well known to them, leading through all these mountains, and we could not get upon one where they would not be sure to head us, and you know they say they have spies continually out to let the tribe know when any of their enemies come into the vicinity of their village."

M. A. "Well, Olive, how often have you told me that were it not for a very faint hope you have of getting away, and your concern for me, you would rather die than live. And you know we both think they intend to sell us, and if they sell us to these Mohaves we will have to travel three hundred miles, and I can never live through it. I have a severe cough now, and almost every night I take more cold. Ma always said 'her Mary Ann would die with consumption,' but she did not think, I guess, of such a consumption as this."

"Poor girl," thought Olive, half aloud, "how her eyes glisten, how her cheeks every day become more spare and pale, and her black, flashing eye is sinking into her head." Olive turned her head carelessly, wiped the tear from her eye, and looking again in the upturned face of her sister, said: "Why, Mary, if you are afraid that you would perish in traveling to the Mohave country, how could you stand the roving day and night among the hills, and we should be obliged, you know, to travel away from the trail for a week, perhaps a month, living on roots?"

M. A. "As for roots, they are about all we get now, and I had rather live on them in trying to get away than in staying here, or being driven like oxen again three hundred miles."

By this time the little pale face of her sister kindled with such an enthusiasm that Olive could hardly avoid expressing the effect it had upon her own mind. Mary was about to continue when her sister, seeing an Indian near them, bade her hush, and they were about to renew their work when Mary said: "Look! who are those? they are Indians, they are those very Mohaves! See! they have a horse, and there is a squaw among them."

The Indian, who was approaching them, had by this time caught a view of them, and was running to camp to spread the news. "I had," says the older, "now no doubt that the approaching company were Mohaves, and I was half inclined to improve the excitement and carelessness that would prevail for a while after their coming among us, to slip away, taking good care to make sure of a piece of meat, a few roots, and something to kill myself with if I should find myself about falling into the hands of pursuers. But in more sober moments we thought it well that this fear of being again caught, and of torture they would be sure to inflict, if we should be unsuccessful, kept us from such a desperate step. The Mohave party are now descending a slope to the Apache village, and roaring, yelling, and dancing prevail through the gathering crowd of Apaches. The party consisted of five men, and a young woman under twenty years. It was not long ere two of the chiefs came to us, and told us that these Mohaves had come after us, according to a contract made with them at a previous visit; that the party had been back to obtain the sanction of Espaniole, the Mohave chief, to the contract, and that now the chief had sent his own

Reception of the two Girls at the Apache Village

daughter to witness to his desire to purchase the white captives. The chief had, however, left it with his daughter to approve or annul the contract that had been made."

This daughter of the chief was a beautiful, mild, and sympathizing woman. Hier conduct and behavior toward these Apache captives bespoke a tutoring, and intelligence, and sweetness of disposition that won their interest at once. She could use the Apache language with fluency, and was thus enabled to talk with the captives for whom she had come. She told her designs to them, and had soon settled it in her mind to approve the contract previously made. During that evening there was much disquiet and misrule throughout the village. The agitated and interested captives, though having been informed that all the negotiations had been completed for their transfer, were much perplexed to learn the reasons of the excitement still raging. There was a studied effort, which was plainly perceived by them, to cover the matter of the councils and heated debates, which occupied the whole night from them; but, by remarks which reached them from different ones, they learned that their destiny was in a very critical suspense. There was a strong party who were angrily opposed to the acceptance of the Mohave propositions, among whom were the murderers of the Oatman family.

Different ones sought by every possible means to draw out the feelings of their captives to the proposed removal. One in particular, a young Indiaii woman, who had forced a disagreeable intimacy with Olive, sought to make her say that she would rather go to the Mohaves. The discretion of the captive girl, however, proved equal to the treachery of the Indian mistress, and no words of complaint, or expressions of desire, could the latter glean to make a perverted report of at head–quarters. The artful Miss To–aquin had endeavored from the first, under friendly pretenses, to acquaint herself with the American language, and succeeded in acquiring a smattering of it. But her eaves–dropping propensities had made the intended victims of her treachery wary, since they had known, in several instances, of her false reports and tale–bearings to the chief.

While sitting alone by a small fire in their wigwam, late in the night, this Jezebel came and seated herself by them, and with her smiles and rattling tongue, feigning an anxious interest in their welfare, said, in substance:

"I suppose you are glad you are going to the Mohaves? But I always hated them; they will steal, and lie, and cheat. Do you think you will get away? I suppose you do. But these miserable Mohaves are going to sell you to another tribe; if they do not, it will not be long ere they will kill you. O, I am very sad because you are going away! I hoped to see you free in a short time; but I know you will never get back to the whites now. Suppose you will try, will you not?"

Olive replied: "We are captives, and since our parents and all our kindred are dead, it matters little where we are, there or here. We are treated better than we deserve, perhaps; and we shall try to behave well, let them treat us as they may; and as to getting away, you know it would be impossible and foolish for us to try."

"The Mohave party professed that it was out of kindness to us that they had come to take us with them; that they knew of the cruel treatment we were suffering among the Apaches, and intended to use us well.

"This would all have been very comforting to us, and it was only to us they made this plea, had we been prepared to give them credit for the absence of that treachery which had been found, so far, as natural to an Indian as his breath. But their natures do not grow sincerity, and their words are to have no weight in judging of their characters. To us it was only gloom that lay upon our way, whether to the Mohaves or to stay in our present position. Their real design it was useless to seek to read until its execution came.

"Sunrise, which greeted us ere we had a moment's sleep, found the party prepared to leave, and we were coolly informed by our captors that we must go with them. Two horses, a few vegetables, a few pounds of beads, and three blankets we found to be our price in that market.

"We found that there were those among the Apaches who were ready to tear us in pieces when we left, and they only wanted a few more to unite with them, to put an end to our lives at once. They now broke forth in the most insulting language to us, and to the remainder of the tribe for bargaining us away. Some laughed, a few among the children, who had received a care and attention from us denied by their natural parents, cried, and a general pow–wow rent the air as we started upon another three hundred miles' trip."

CHAPTER IV

The Journey of three hundred and fifty Miles to the Mohave Valley–The Means of Subsistence during the Time–The Conduct of the Mohaves compared with the Apaches–Arrive at the Valley–The Village–The Chief's Residence–Their Joy at the Returni of Topeka, their Daughter–The Greeting of the new Captives–One Year of Labor and Suffering–The Overflowing of the Colorado–Their Dependence upon it–Their Habits–Cultivation of the Soil–Scarcity of Provisions–Starvation–Mary Ann–Her Decline–Olive's Care, Grief, and Efforts to save her life–Dies of Famine–Many of the Indian Children die–Burial of Mary Ann–The Sympathy and Sorrow of the Chief's Wife.

"We were informed at the outset that we had three hundred and fifty miles before us, and all to be made on foot. Our route we soon found to be in no way preferable to the one by which the Apache village had been reached. It was now about the first day of March, 1852. One year had been spent by us in a condition the most abject, the most desolate, with treatment the most cruel that barbarity and hate could invent, and this all endured without the privilege of a word from ourselves to turn the scale in this direction or that, in a rugged, rocky country, filled with bare mountains or lesser hills with slight vegetation, and that tame and tasteless, or irregular piles of boulders and gravel beds; we were now being hurried on under Indian guardianship alone, we knew not where nor for what purpose. We had not proceeded far ere it was painfully impressed upon our feet, if not our aching hearts, that this trail to a second captivity was no improvement on the first, whatever might be the fate awaiting us at its termination. We had been under tutorage for one whole year in burden bearing, and labor even beyond our strength, but a long walk or run, as this proved, we had not been driven to during that time.

"Mary Ann, poor girl, entered upon this trip with less strength or fortitude to encounter its hardships than the one before. She had not proceeded far before I saw plainly that she would not be able to stand it long. With the many appearances of kindness that our present overseers put on, yet they seemed to be utterly destitute of any heart or will to enter into the feelings of those who had been brought up more delicately than themselves, or to understand their inability to perform the task dictated by their rough and hardy habits. Our feet soon became sore, and we were unable, on the second day after about noon, to keep up with their rapid pace. A small piece of meat was put into our hands on starting, and this with the roots we were allowed to dig, and these but few, was our sole subsistence for ten days.

"With much complaining, and some threatening from our recent captors, we were allowed to rest on the second day a short time. After this we were not compelled to go more than thirty–five miles any one day, and pieces of skins were furnished for our feet, but not until they had been needlessly bruised and mangled without them. The nights were cool, and, contrary to our expectations, the daughter of the chief showed us kindness throughout the journey by sharing her blankets with us at each camp.

"Of all rough, uncouth, irregular, and unattractive countries through which human beings trail, the one through which that ten days' march led us, must remain unsurpassed.

"On the eleventh day, about two hours before sunset, we made a bold steep ascent (and of such we had been permitted to climb many) from which we had an extensive view on either side.

"Before us, commencing a little from the foot of our declivity, lay a narrow valley covered with a carpet of green, stretching a distance, seemingly, of twenty miles. On either side were the high, irregularly sloped mountains, with their foot hills robed in the same bright green as the valley, and with their bald humpbacks and sharp peaks, treeless, verdureless, and desolate, as if the tempests of ages had poured their rage upon their sides and summits.

"Our guides soon halted. We immediately observed by their movements and mnanifestations that some object beyond the loveliness that nature had strewn upon that valley, was enrapturing their gaze. We had stood gazing a few moments only, when the smoke at the distance of a few miles, winding in gentle columns up the ridges, spoke to us of the abodes or tarrying of human beings. Very soon there came into the field of our steady view a large number of huts, clothing the valley in every direction. We could plainly see a large cluster of these huts huddled into a nook in the hills on our right and on the bank of a river, whose glassy waters threw the sunlight in our face; its winding, zigzag course pointed out to us by the row of beautiful cottonwood trees that thickly studded its vicinity.

"'Here, Olive,' said Mary Ann, 'is the place where they live. O isn't it a beautiful valley? It seems to me I should like to live here.'

"'May be,' said I, 'that you will not want to go back to the whites ally more.'

"'O yes, there is green grass and fine meadows there, besides good people to care for us; these savages are enough to make any place look ugly, after a little time.'

"We were soon ushered into the 'Mollave Valley,' and had not proceeded far before we began to pass the low, rude huts of the Mohave settlers.

They greeted us with shouts, and dance, and song as we passed. Our guides kept up, however, a steady in heeding march for the village, occasionally joined by fierce, filthy–looking Mohaves, and their more filthy–looking children, who would come up, look rudely in our faces, fasten their deep–set, small, flashing eyes upon us, and trip along, with merrymaking, hallooing, and dancing at our side.

"We were conducted immediately to the home of the chief, and welcomed with the staring eyes of collecting groups, and an occasional smile from the members of the chief's family, who gave the warmnest expressions of joy over the return of their daughter and sister so long absent. Seldom does our civilization furnish a more hearty exhibition of affection for kindred, than welcomed the coming in of this member of the chief's family, though she had been absent but a few days. The chief's house was on a beautiful but small elevation crowning the river bank, from which the eye could sweep a large section of the valley, and survey the entire village, a portion of which lined each bank of the stream.

"As a model, and one that will give a correct idea of the form observed, especially in their village structures, we may speak of the chief's residence. When we reached the outskirts of the town we observed upon the bank of the river a row of beautiful cottonwood trees, just putting out their new leaves and foliage, their branches interlocking, standing in a row, about a perfect square of about one hundred feet, and arranged in taste. They were thrifty, and seemed fed from a rich soil, and with other plots covered with the same growths, and abounding throughout the village, presented truly an oasis in the general desert of country upon which we had been trailing our painful walk for the last ten days, climbing and descending, with unshapen rocks, and sharp gravel, and burning sands for our pavement. Immediately behind the row of trees first spoken of, was a row of poles or logs, each about six inches in diameter and standing close to each other, one end firmly set in the ground and reaching up about twenty feet, forming an inclosure of about fifty feet square.

"We entered this inclosure through a door, (never shut,) and found a tidy yard, grass–plotted. Inside of this was still another inclosure of about twenty feet, walled by the same kind of fence, only about one third as high. Running from front to rear, and dividing this dwelling–place of the Mohave magnate into equal parts, stood a row of these logs stuck in the ground, and running up about three feet above the level top of the outside row, and forming a ridge for the resting of the roof. The roof was a thick mat of limbs and mud. A few blankets, a small smoking fire near the door, with naked walls over which the finishing Sand of the upholsterer had never passed, a floor made when all *terra firma* was created, welcomed us to the interior.

"The daughter of the chief had been kind to us, if kindness could be shown under their barbarous habits and those rates of travel while on our way. She was more intelligent and seemed capable of more true sympathy and affection, than any we had yet met in our one year's exile. She was of about seventeen years, sprightly, jovial, and good–natured, and at times manifested a deep sympathy for us, and a commiseration of our desolate condition. But though she was daughter of the chief, their habits of barbarousness could not bend to courtesy even toward those of rank. She had walked the whole distance to the Apaches, carrying a roll of blankets, while two horses were rode by two stalwart, healthy Mohaves by her side.

"On entering the house Topeka, who had accompanied us, gave an immediate and practical evidence that her stinted stomach had not become utterly deaf to all the demands of hunger. Seeing a cake roasting in the ashes, she seized it, and dividing it into three parts, she gave me the Benjamin portion and bade us eat, which was done with greediness and pleasant surprise.

"Night came on and with it the gathering of a large concourse of Indians, their brown, stout wives and daughters,. and swarms of little ones whose faces and bare limbs would have suggested anything else sooner than the near vicinity of clear water, or their knowledge of its use for purifying purposes.

"The Indians were mostly tall, stout, with large heads, broad faces, and of a much more intelligent appearance than the Apaches. Bark–clad, where clad at all, the scarcity of their covering indicating either a warm climate or a great destitution of the clothing material, or something else.

"Their conduct during that night of wild excitement, was very different from that by which our coming among the Apaches was celebrated. That was one of selfish iron–hearted fiends, glutting over a murderous, barbarous deed of death and plunder; this was that of a company of indolent, superstitious, and lazy heathen, adopting the only method which their darkness and ignorance would allow to signify their joy over the return of kindred and the delighted purchase of two foreign captives. They placed us out upon the green, and in the light of a large, brisk fire, and kept up their dancing, singing, jumping, and shouting, until near the break of day.

"After they had dispersed, and that night of tears, and the bitterest emotions, and most torturing remembrances of the past, and reflections of our present had nearly worn away, with bleeding feet, worn in places almost to the bone, with aching limbs, beneath a thin covering, side by side, little Mary Ann and myself lay us down upon a sand bed to meditate upon sleep. A few hours were spent in conversation, conducted in a low whisper, with occasional moments of partial drowsiness, haunted with wild, frantic dreams."

Though five years separate that time and the present, where is the heart but throbs sensitive to the dark, prison–like condition of these two girls. Look at their situation, the scenes around; having reached a strange tribe by a toilsome, painful ten days' journey, the sufferings of which were almost insupportable and life consuming, having been for nearly the whole night of their introduction to a new captivity made the subjects of shouting and confusion, heathenish, indelicate, and indecent, and toward morning hiding themselves under a scanty covering, surrounded by unknown savages; whispering into each other's ears the hopes, fears, and impressions of their new condition. Coveting sleep, but every touch of its soft hand upon their moistened eyelids turned to torture and hideousness by scary visions and dreams; harassed in mind over the uncertainty and doubt haunting their imaginations, as to the probable purposes of their new possessors in all their painstaking to secure a transfer of the captives to them. It is true that less of barbarity had marked the few days of their dependence upon their new owners, than their Apache hardships; but they had sadly learned already that under fiiendly guises their possible treachery might be wrapping and nursing some foul and murderous design.

Plunged now into the depths of a wild country, where the traces of a white foot would be sought in vain for hundreds of miles, and at such a distance from the nearest route of the hurrying emigrant, as to preclude almost the traveling of hope to their exile and gloom; it is no marvel that these few hours allotted to sleep at the latter part of the night, were disturbed by such questions as these: Why have they purchased us? What labor or service do they intend subjecting us to? Have they connived with our former masters to remove us still further from the habitations of our countrymen, and sought to plunge us so deep in these mountain defiles, that they may solace themselves with that insatiate revenge upon our race which will encounter any hardship rather than allow us the happiness of a return to our native land? No marvel that they could not drive away such thoughts, though a lacerated body was praying for balmy sleep, " nature's sweet restorer."

Mary Ann, the youngest, a little girl of eight years, had been declining in health and strength for some time. She had almost starved on that long road, kept up principally by a small piece of meat. For over three hundred miles had she come, climbing rocks, traversing sun–burned gravel and sand, marking the way by bleeding feet, sighs, and piteous moanings; well–nigh breaking the heart of her older sister, whose deepest anguish was the witnessing of these sufferings that she could not relieve. She was not inclined to complain; nay, she was given to a patient reserve that would bear her grief alone, sooner than trouble her loved sister with it. She had from infancy been the favorite child of the family; the only one of a frail constitution, quickest to learn, and best to remember; and often, when at home, and the subject of disease and pain, exhibiting a meekness, judgment, and fortitude beyond her years. She was tenderly loved by the whole family; nursed by her fond mother with a delicacy and concern bestowed on none of the rest; and now bound to the heart of her only sister by a tie strengthened by mutual sufferings, and that made her every woe and sigh a dagger to the heart of Olive. No marvel that the latter should say: "Poor girl, I love her tenderly, ardently; and now to see her driven forth whole days, with declining health, at a pace kept up by these able–bodied Indians; to see her climb rugged cliffs, at times upon her hands and knees, struggling up where others could walk, the sweat coursing down freely from her pearly–white forehead; to hear her heave those half–suppressed sighs; to see the steps of those little bleeding feet totter and falter; to see the big tears standing out of her eyes, glistening as if in the borrowed light of a purer home; to see her turn at times and bury her head in some of the tattered furs wrapped about a part of her person, and weeping alone, and then come to me, saying: 'I How far, dear Olive, must we yet go?' To hear her ask, and ask in vain, for bread, for meat, for water, for something to eat, when nothing but their laziness denied her request; these were sights and scenes I pray God to deliver me from in future! O that I could blot out the impression they have indelibly written upon my mind!

"'But we are now here, and must make the best of it,' was the interruption made the next morning to memories and thoughts like the above. We were narrowly watched, and with an eye and jealousy that seemed to indicate some design beyond and unlike the one that was avowed to move them to purchase us, and to shut out all knowledge of the way back to our race. We found the location and scenery of our new home much pleasanter than the one last occupied. The valley extended about thirty or forty miles, northeast by southwest, and varying from two to five miles in width. Through its whole length flowed the beautiful Colorado, in places a rapid, leaping stream, in others making its way quietly, noiselessly over a deeper bed. It varied, like all streams whose sources are in immediate mountains, in depth, at different seasons of the year. During the melting of the snows that clothed the mountain–tops to the north, when we came among the Mohaves, it came roaring and thundering along its rock–bound banks, threatening the whole valley, and doing some damage.

"We found the Mohaves accustomed to the tillage of the soil to a limited extent, and in a peculiar way. And it was a season of great rejoicing when the Colorado overflowed, as it was only after overflows that they could rely upon their soil for a crop. In the autumn they planted the wheat carefully in hills with their fingers and in the spring they planted corn, melons, and a few garden vegetables. They had, however, but a few notions, and these were crude, about agriculture. They were utterly without skill or art in any useful calling. When we first arrived among them the wheat sown the previous fall had come up, and looked green and thrifty, though it did not appear, nor was it, sufficient to maintain one–fifth of their population. They spent more time in raising twenty spears of wheat from one hill, than was necessary to have cultivated one acre, with the improvenents they might and should have learned in the method of doing it. It was to us, however, an enlivening sight to see even these scattered parcels of grain growing, clothing sections of their valley. It was a remembrancer, and reminded us of home, (now no more ours,) and placed us in a nearness to the customs of a civilized mode of life that we had not realized before.

"For a time after coming among them but little was said to us; none seemed desirous to enter into any intercourse, or inquire even, if it had been possible for us to understand them, as to our welfare, past or present. Topeka gave us to know that we were to remain in their house. Indeed we were merely regarded as strange intruders, with whom they had no sympathy, and their bearing for a while toward us seemed to say: 'You may live here if you can eke out an existence, by bowing yourselves unmurmuringly to our barbarism and privations.'

"In a few days they began to direct us to work in various ways, such as bringing wood and water, and to perform various errands of convenience to them. Why they took the course they did I have never been able to imagine; but it was only by degrees that their exactions were enforced. We soon learned, however, that our condition was that of unmitigated slavery, not to the adults merely, but to the children. In this respect it was very much as among the Apaches. Their whimpering, idiotic children, of not half a dozen years, very soon learned to drive us about with all the authority of an Eastern lord. And these filthy creatures would go in quest of occasions, seemingly to gratify their love of command; and any want of hurried attention to them was visited upon us by punishment, either by whipping or the withholding of our food. Besides, the adults of the tribe enjoyed the sport of seeing us thus forced into submission to their children.

"The Colorado had overflown during the winter, and there had been considerable rain. The Mohaves were in high hopes for a bountiful crop during this season. What was to them a rich harvest would be considered in Yankee land, or in the Western states, a poor compensation for so much time and plodding labor. For two years before they had raised but little. Had the industry and skill of the least informed of our agriculturists been applied to this Mohave valley, it might have been made as productive and fruitful a spot as any I ever saw. But they were indolent and lazy, so that it would seem impossible for ingenuity to invent modes by which they might work to a greater disadvantage, or waste the little of strength they did use. While their lot had cast them into the midst of superior natural advantages, which ought to have awakened their pride and ambition to do something for themselves, yet they were indisposed to every fatiguing toil, unless in the chase or war."

Nothing during the summer of 1852 occurred to throw any light upon that one question, to these captive girls the all–absorbing one, one which, like an everywhere present spirit, haunted them day and night, as to the probabilities of their ever escaping from Indian captivity. It was not long before their language, of few words, was so far understood as to make it easy to understand the Mohaves in conversation. Every day brought to their ears expressions, casually dropped, showing their spite and hate to the white race. They would question their captives closely, seeking to draw from them any discontent they might feel in their present condition. They taunted them, in a less ferocious manner than the Apaches, but with every evidence of an equal hate, about the good–for–nothing whites.

"At times, when some of their friends were visiting in the neighborhood of our valley, they would call for the captives that they might see them. One day, while one of the sub–chiefs and his family were visiting at Espaniola's house, Mary and I were out a little from the house singing, and were overheard. This aroused their curiosity, and we were called, and many questions were put to us as to what we were singing, where we learned to sing, and if the whites were good singers. Mary and I, at their request, sang them some of our Sabbath–school hymns, and some of the short children's songs we had learned. After this we were teased very much to sing to them. Several times a small string of beads was made up among them and presented to us for singing to them for two or three hours; also pieces of red flannel, (an article that to them was the most valuable of any they could possess,) of which after some time we had several pieces. These we managed to attach together with ravelings, and wore them upon our persons. The beads we wore about our necks, squaw fashion."

Many of them were anxious to learn the language of the whites; among these one Ccearekae, a young man of some self–conceit and pride. He asked the elder of the girls, "How do you like living with the Mohaves?" To which she replied, "I do not like it so well as among the whites, for we do not have enough to eat."

Cceareke. "We have enough to satisfy us; you Americanos (a term also by them learned of the Mexicans) work hard, and it does you no good; we enjoy ourselves."

Olive. "Well, we enjoy ourselves well at home, and all our white people seem happier than any Indian I have seen since."

Ccearekae. Our great fathers worked just as you whites do, and they had many nice things to wear; but the flood came and swept the old folks away, and a white son of the family stole all the arts, with the clothing, etc., and the Mohaves have had none since."

Olive. "But if our people had this beautiful valley they would till it, and raise much grain. You Mohaves don't like to work, and you say you do not have enough to eat; then it is because you are lazy."

"At this his wrath was aroused, and with angry words and countenance he left. I frequently told them how grain, and cattle, and fowls would abound, if such good land was under the control of the whites. This would sometimes kindle their wrath, and flirts, and taunts, and again at other times their curiosity. One day several of them were gathered, and questioning about our former homes, and the white nation, and the way by which a living was made, etc. I told them of plowing the soil. They then wanted to see the figure of a plow. I accordingly, with sticks and marks in the sand, made as good a plow as a girl of fifteen would be expected, perhaps, to make out of such material; drew the oxen and hitched them to my plow, and told them how it would break the soil. This feasted their curiosity a while, but ended in a volley of scorn and mockery to me and the race of whites, and a general outburst of indignant taunts about their meanness.

"They were very anxious to know how breaking up of the soil would make grain grow; of what use it was; whether women labored in raising grain. We told them of milking the cows, and how our white people mowed the grass and fattened cattle, and many other things, to which they gave the ear of a curiosity plainly beyond what they wanted us to understand they cared about it.

"I told them of the abundance that rewards white labor, while they had so little. They said:'Your ancestors were dishonest, and their children are weak, and that by and by the pride and good living of the present whites would ruin them. You whites, 'continued they,'have forsaken nature and want to possess the earth, but you will not be able.' In thus conversing with them I learned of a superstition they hold as to the origin of the distinction existing among the red and white races.

"It was as follows: They said, pointing to a high mountain at the northern end of the valley, (the highest in the vicinity,) there was once a flood in ancient time that covered all the world but that mountain, and all the present races then were merged in one family, and this family was saved from the general deluge by getting upon that mountain. They said that this antediluvian family was very large, and had great riches, clothing, cattle, horses, and much to eat. They said that after the water subsided one of the family took all the cattle and our kind of clothing, and went north, was turned from red to white, and so there settled. That another part of this family took deer skins and bark, and from these the Indians came. They held that this ancient family were all of red complexion until the progenitor of the whites stole, then he was turned white. They said the Hiiccos (dishonest whites) would lose their cattle yet; that this thieving would turn upon themselves. They said remains of the old' big house,' in which this ancient family lived, were up there yet; also pieces of bottles, broken dishes, and remnants of all the various kinds of articles used by them.

"We. were told by them that this venerated spot had, ever since the flood, been the abode of spirits; (Hippoweka, the name for spirit;) and that these spirits were perfectly acquainted with all the doings, and even the secret motives and character, of each individual of the tribe. And also that it was a place consecrated to these spirits, and if the feet of mortals should presume to tread this enchanted spirit–land, a fire would burst from the mountain and instantly consume them, except it be those who are selected and appointed by these spirits to communicate some special message to the tribe. This favored class were generally the physicians of the tribe. And when a war project was designed by these master spirits, they signified the bloody intention by causing the mountains to shoot forth lurid tongues of fire, visible only to the revelators. All their war plans and the time of their execution, their superstition taught them, were conmmunicated by the flame–lit pinnacle to those depositories of the will of the spirits, and by them, under professed superhuman dictation, the time, place, object, and method of the war were communicated to the chief. Yet the power of the chief was absolute, and when his practical wisdom suggested, these wizards always found a license by a second consultation to modify the conflict, or change the time and method of its operation.

"It was their belief that in the region of this mountain there was held in perpetual chains the spirit of every 'Hicco'–that they had been successful in slaying; and that the souls of all such were there eternally doomed to torment of the fiercest quenchless fires, and the Mohave by whose hand the slaughter was perpetrated, would be exalted to eternal honors and superior privileges therefor.

"It was with strange emotions, after listening to this superstitious tale, that our eyes rested upon that old bald peak, and saw within the embrace of its internal fires, the spirits of many of our own race, and thought of their being bound by this Mohave legend to miseries so extreme, and woes so unmitigated, and a revenge so insatiate.

"But according to their belief we could only expect a like fate by attempting their rescue, and we did not care enough for the professed validness of their faith to risk companionship with them, even for the purpose of attempting to unbind the chains of their tormenting bondage; and we turned away, most heartily pitying them for their subjection to so gross a superstition, without any particular concern for those who had been appointed by its authority to its vengeance. We felt that if the Hiiccos could manage to escape all other hells, they could manage this one without our sympathy or help.

"There was little game in the Mohave Valley, and of necessity little meat was used by this tribe. At some seasons of the year, winter and spring, they procure fish firom a small lake in the vicinity. This was a beautiful little body of water at freshet seasons, but in the dry seasons became a loathsome mudhole. In their producing season, the Mohaves scarcely raised a four months' supply, yet they might have raised for the whole year as well. Often I thought, as I saw garden vegetables and grain plucked ere they were grown, to be devoured by these lazy'live to–day' savages, I should delight to see the hand of the skillful agriculturist upon that beautiful valley, with the Mohaves standing by to witness its capabilities for producing.

"We spent most of this summer in hard work. We were, for a long time, roused at the break of day, baskets were swung upon our shoulders, and we were obliged to go from six to eight miles for the 'Musquite,' a seed or berry growing upon a bush about the size of our Manzanita. In the first part of the season, this tree bloomed a beautiful flower, and after a few weeks a large seed–bud could be gathered from it, and this furnished what is truly to be called their staple article of subsistence. We spent from twilight to twilight again, for a long time, in gathering this. And often we found it impossible, from its scarcity that year, to fill our basket in a day, as we were required; and for failing to do this we seldom escaped a chastisement. This seed, when gathered, was hung up in their huts to be thoroughly dried, and to be used when their vegetables and grain should be exhausted. I could endure myself, the task daily assigned me, but to see the demands and exactions made upon little Mary Ann, day after day, by these unfeeling wretches, as many of them were, when her constitution was already broken down, and she daily suffering the most excruciating pains from the effects of barbarity she had already received; this was a more severe trial than all I had to perform of physical labor. And I often felt as though it would be a sad relief to see her sink into the grave, beyond the touch and oppression of the ills and cruel treatment she was subjected to. But there were times when she would enliven after rest, which from her utter inability they were obliged to grant.

"We were accused by our captors several times during this season, of designing and having plotted already to make our escape. Some of them would frequently question and annoy us much to discover, if possible, our feelings and our intentions in reference to our captivity. Though we persisted ill denying any purpose to attempt our escape, many of themll seemed to disbelieve us, and would warn us against any such undertaking, by assuring us they would follow us, if it were necessary, quite to the white settlements, and would torment us in the most painful manner, if we were ever to be recaptured.

"One day, while we were sitting in the hut of the chief, having just returned from a root–digging excursion, there came two of their physicians attended by the chief and several others, to the door of the hut. The chief's wife then bade us go out upon the yard, and told us that the physicians were going to put marks on our faces. It was with much difficulty that we could understand, however, at first, what was their design. We soon, however, by the motions accompanying the commands of the wife of the chief, came to understand that they were going to tatoo our faces.

"We had seen them do this to some of their female children, and we had often conversed with each other about expressing the hope that we should be spared from receiving their marks upon us. I ventured to plead with them for a few moments that they would not put those ugly marks upon our faces. But it was in vain. To all our expostulations they only replied in substance that they knew why we objected to it; that we expected to return to the whites, and we would be ashamed of it then; but that it was their resolution we should never return, and that as we be longed to them we should wear their 'Ki–e–chook.' They said further, that if we should get away, and they should find us among other tribes, or if some other tribes should steal us, they would by this means know us.

"They then pricked the skin in small regular rows on our chins with a very sharp stick, until they bled freely. They then dipped these same sticks in the juice of a certain weed that grew on the banks of the river, and then in the powder of a blue stone that was to be found in low water, in some places along the bed of the stream, (the stone they first burned until it would pulverize easy, and in burning it turned nearly black,) and pricked this fine powder into these lacerated parts of the face.

"The process was somewhat painful, though it pained us more for two or three days after than at the time of its being done. They told us this could never be taken from the face, and that they had given us a different mark from the one worn by their own females, as we saw, but the same with which they marked all their own captives, and that they could claim us in whatever tribe they might find us.

"The autumn was by far the easiest portion of the year for us. To multiply words would not give any clearer idea to the reader of our condition. It was one continual routine of drudgery. Toward spring their grains were exhausted. There was but little rain, not enough to raise the Colorado near the top of its banks. The Mohaves became very uneasy about their wheat in the ground. It came up much later than usual, and looked sickly and grew tardily after it was out of the ground. It gave a poor, wretched promise at the best for the next year. Ere it was fairly up there were not provisions or articles of any kind to eat in the village any one night to keep its population two days. We found that the people numbered really over fifteen hundred. We were now driven forth every morning by the first break of day, cold and sometimes damp, with rough, bleak winds, to glean the old, dry musquite seed that chanced to have escaped the fatiguing search of the summer and autumn months. From this on to the time of gathering the scanty harvest of that year, we were barely able to keep soul and body together. And the return for all our vigorous labor was a little dry seed in small quantities. And all this was put forth under the most sickening apprehensions of a worse privation awaiting us the next year. This harvest was next to nothing. No rain had fallen during the spring to do much good.

"Above what was necessary for seeding again, there was not one month's supply when harvest was over. We had gathered less during the summer of 'musquite,' and nothing but starvation could be expected. This seemed to throw the sadness of despair upon our condition, and to blot all our faint but fond hopes of reaching our native land. We knew, or thought we knew, that in case of an extremity our portion must be mneted out after these voracious, unfeeling idlers had supplied tlhemselves. We had already seen that a calamity or adversity had the effect to make these savages more savage and implacable. I felt more keenly for Mary Ann than myself'. She often said (for we were already denied the larger half necessary to satisfy our appetites) that she'could not live long without something more to eat.' She would speak of the plenty that she had at home, and that might now be there, and sometimes would rather chide me for making no attempts to escape. 'O, if I could only get one dish of bread and milk,' she would frequently say, 'I could enjoy it so well!' They ground their seed between stones, and with water made a mush, and we spent many mournftil hours of conversation over our gloomy state as we Saw the supply of this tasteless, nauseating *'musquite mush'* failing, and that the season of our almost sole dependence upon it was yet but begun.

"It was not infrequent that a death occurred among them by the neglect and laziness so characteristic of the Indian. One day I was out gathering chottatoe, when I was suddenly surprised and fright ened by running upon one of the victims of this stupid, barbarous inhumanity. He was a tall, bony Indian of about thirty years. His eye was rather sunken, his visage marred, as if he had passed through extreme hardships. He was lying upon the ground, moaning and rolling from side to side in agony the most acute and intense. I looked upon him, and my heart was moved with pity. Little Mary said,'I will go up and find out what ails him.' On inquiry we soon found that he had been for some time ill, but not so as to become utterly helpless. And not until one of their number is entirely disabled, do they seem to manifest any feeling or concern for him. The physician was called, and soon decided that he was not in the least diseased. He told Mary that nothing ailed him save the want of food; said that he had been unable for some time to procure his food; that his friends devoured any that was brought into camp without dividing it with him; that he had been gradually running down, and now he wanted to die. O there was such dejection, such a forlorn, despairing look written upon llis countenance as made an impression upon my mind which is yet vivid and mournful.

"He soon died, and then his father and all his relatives commenced a hideous, barbarous howling and jumping, indicative of the most poignant grief. Whether their sorrowing was a matter of conscience or bereavement, none could tell, but it would im prove my opinion of them to believe it originated with the former.

"Such scenes were not far between, and yet these results of their laziness and want of enterprise and humanity, when thickening upon them, had no effect to beget a different policy or elevate them to that life of happiness, thrift, and love which would have prolonged their years, and removed the dismal, gloomy aspect of every–day life among them.

"We were now put upon a stinted allowance, and the restrictions upon us were next to the taking the life of Mary Ann. During the second autumn, and at the time spoken of above, the chief's wife gave us some seed–grain, corn and wheat, showed us about thirty feet square of ground marked off upon which we might plant it and raise something for ourselves. We planted our wheat, and carefully concealed the handful of corn and melon–seeds to plant in the spring. This we enjoyed very much. It brought to our minds the extended grain–fields that waved about our cottage in Illinois, of the beautiful spring when winter's ice and chill had departed before the breath of a warmer season, of the May–mornings, when we had gone forth to the plow–fields and followed barefooted in the new–turned furrow, and of the many long days of grain–growing and ripening in which we had watched the daily change in the fields of wheat and oats.

"These hours of plying our fingers (not sewing) in the ground flew quickly by, but not without their tears and forebodings that ere we could gather the results, famine might lay our bodies in the dust. Indeed we could see no means by which we could possibly maintain ourselves to harvest again. Winter, a season of sterility and frozen nights, was fast approaching, and to add to my desolateness, I plainly saw that grief, or want of food, or both, were slowly and inch by inch, enfeebling and wasting away Mary Ann.

"The Indians said that about sixty miles away there was a'Taneta' (tree) that bore a berry called 'Oth–to–toa,' upon which they had subsisted for some time several years before, but it could be reached only by a mountainous and wretched way of sixty miles. Soon a large party made preparations and set out in quest of this 'life–preserver.' Many of those accustomed to bear burdens were not able to go. Mary Ann started, but soon gave out and returned. A few Indians accompanied us, but it was a disgrace for them to bear burdens; this was befitting only to squaws and captives. I was commanded to pick up my basket and go with them, and it was only with much pleading I could get them to spare my sister the undertaking when she gave out. I had borne that 'Chliechucek' empty and full over many hundred miles, but never over so rugged a way, nor when it seemed so heavy as now.

"We reached the place on the third day, and found the taineta to be a bush, anid very much resembling the mintsquite, only with a much larger leaf. It grew to a height of from five to thirty feet. The berry was much more pleasant to the taste than the musquite; the juice of it, when extracted and mixed with water, was very much like the orange. The tediousness and perils of this trip were very much enlivened with the hope of getting something with which to nourish and prolong the life of Mary. She was very much depressed, and appeared quite ill when I left her.

"After wandering about for two days with but little gathered, six of us started in quest of some place where the oth–to–toa might be more abundant. We traveled over twenty miles away from our temporary camp. We found tanetas in abundance, and loaded with the berry. We had reached a field of them we judged never found before.

"Our baskets being filled, we hastened to join the camp party before they should start for the village. We soon lost our way, the night being dark, and wandered without water the whole night, and were nearly all sick from eating our oth–to–toa berry. Toward day, nearly exhausted, and three of our number very sick, we were compelled to halt. We watched over and nursed the sick, sweating them with the medical leaf always kept with us, and about the only medicine used by the Mohaves. But our efforts were vain, for before noon the three had breathed their last. A fire was kindled and their bodies were burned; and for several hours I expected to be laid upon one of those funeral pyres in that deep, dark, and almost trackless wilderness.

"I think I suffered more during those two or three hours in mind and body than at any other period of my captivity in the same time. We feared to stay only as long as was necessary, for our energies were well–nigh exhausted. We started back, and I then saw an Indian carry a basket. One of them took the baskets of the dead, and kept up with us. The rest of our party went howling through the woods in the most dismal manner. The next day we found the camp, and found we had been nearly around it. We were soon on our way, and by traveling all one night we were at the village.

"It would be impossible to put upon paper any true idea of my feelings and sufferings during this trip, on account of Mary. Had it not been for her I could have consented to have laid down and died with the three we buried. I did not then expect to get back. I feared she would not live, and I found on reaching the village that she had materially failed, and had been furnished with scarcely food enough to keep her alive. I sought by every possible care to recruit her, and for a short time she revived. The berry we had gathered, while it would add to one's flesh, and give an appearance of healthiness, (if the stomach could bear it,) had but little strengthening properties in it.

"I traveled whole days together in search of the eggs of blackbirds for Mary Ann. These eggs at seasons were plenty, but not then. These she relished very much. I cherished for a short time the hope that she might, by care and nursing, be kept up until spring, when we could get fish. The little store we had brought in was soon greedily devoured, and with the utmost difficulty could we get a morsel. The ground was searched for miles, and every root that could nourish human life was gathered. The Indians became reckless and quarrelsome, and with unpardonable selfishness each would struggle for his own life in utter disregard of his fellows. Mary Ann failed fast. She and I were whole days at a time without anything to eat; when by some chance, or the kindness of the chief's daughter, we would get a morsel to satisfy our cravings. Often would Mary say to me, I am well enough, but I want something to eat; then I should be well.' I could not leave her over night. Roots there were none I could reach by day and return; and when brought in, our lazy lords would take them for their own children. Several children had died, and more were in a dying state. Each death that occurred was the occasion of a night or day of frantic howling and crocodile mourning. Mary was weak and growing weaker, and I gave up in despair. I sat by her side for a few days, most of the time only begging of the passers–by to give me something to keep Mary alive. Sometimes I succeeded. Had it not been for the wife and daughter of the chief, we could have obtained nothing. They seemed really to feet for us, and I have no doubt would have done more if in their power. My sister would not complain, but beg for something to eat.

"She would often think and speak in the most affectionate manner of'dear pa and ma,' and with confidence she would say,'they suffered an awful death, but they are now safe and happy in a better and brighter land, though I am left to starve among savages.' She seemed now to regard life no longer as worth preserving, and she kept constantly repeating expressions of longing to die and be removed fromn a gloomy captivity to a world where 1no tear of sorrow dims the eye of innocence and beauty. She called me to her side one day and said: 'Olive, I shall die soon; you will live and get away. Father and mother have got through with sufferings, and are now at rest; I shall soon be with them and those dear brothers and sisters.' She then asked me to sing, and she joined her sweet, clear voice, without faltering, with me, and we tried to sing the evening hymn we had been taught at the family altar:

'The day is past and gone,
The evening sliades appear,' etc.

"My grief was too great. The struggling emotions of my mind I tried to keep from her, but could not. She said: 'Don't grieve for me; I have been a care to you all the while. I don't like to leave you here all alone, but God is with you, and our heavenly Father will keep and comfort those who trust in him. O, I am so glad that we were taught to love and serve the Saviour.' She then asked me to sing the hymn commencing:

'I How tedious and tasteless the hours
When Jesus no longer I see.'

"I tried to sing, but could not get beyond the first line. But it did appear that visions of a bright world were hers, as with a clear, unfaltering strain she sang the entire hymn. She gradually sank away without much pain, and all the time happy. She had not spent a day in our captivity without asking God to pardon, to bless, and to save. I was faint, and unable to stand upon my feet long at a time. My cravings for food were almost uncontrollable; and at the same time, among unfeeling savages, to watch her gradual but sure approach to the vale of death, from want of food that their laziness alone prevented us having in abundance, this was a time and scene upon which I can only gaze with horror, and the very remembrance of which I would blot out if I could.

"She lingered thus for several days. She suffered much, mostly from hunger. Often did I hear, as I sat near her weeping, some Indian coming near break out in a rage, because I was permitted to spend my time thus with her; that they had better kill Mary, then I could go, as I ought to be made to go, and dig roots and procure food for the rest of them.

"O what moments, what hours were these! Every object in all the fields of sight seemed to wear a horrid gloom.

"One day, during her singing, quite a crowd gathered about her and seemed much surprised. Some of them would stand for whole hours and gaze upon her countenance as if enchained by a strange sight, and this while some of their own kindred were dying in other parts of the village. Among these was the wife of the chief, 'Aespaneo.' I ought here to say that neither that woman nor her daughter ever gave us any unkind treatment. She came up one day, hearing Mary sing, and bent for some time silently over her. She looked in her face, felt of her, and suddenly broke out in a most piteous lamentation. She wept, and wept from the heart and aloud. I never saw a parent seem to feel more keenly over a dying child. She sobbed, she moaned, she howled. And thus bending over and weeping she stood the whole night. The next morning, as I sat near my sister, shedding my tears in my hands, she called me to her side and said:'I am willing to die. O, I shall be so nmuchl bettelr off thlele!' and]her strength failed. She tried to sing, but wvas too weak.

DEATH OF MARY ANN AT THE INDIAN CAMP

'A number of thle tribe, men, women, and children, were about her, the chlief's wife watching her everv moment. She died in a few moments after her dying words quoted above.

"She sank to the sleep of death as quietly as sinks the innocent infant to sleep in its mother's arms.

When I saw that she was dead, I could but give myself up to loneliness, to wailing and despair. 'The last of our family dead, and all of them by tortures inflicted by Indian savages,' I exclaimed to myself. I went to her and tried to find remaining life, but no pulse, no breatth was there. I could but adore the mercy that had so wisely thrown a vail of concealnment over these three years of affliction. Had their scenes been mapped out to be read beforehand, and to be received step by step, as they were really meted out to us, no heart could have sustained them.

"I wished and most earnestly desired that I might at once lie down in the same cold, icy embrace that I saw fast stiffening the delicate limbs of that dear sister.

"I reasoned at times, that die I must and soon, and that I had the right to end my sufferings at once, and prevent these savages by cold, cruel neglect, murdering me by the slow tortures of a starvation that had already its score of victims in our village. The only heart that shared my woes was now still, the only heart (as I then supposed) that survived the massacre of seven of our family group was now cold in death, and why should I remain to feel the gnawings of hunger and pain a few days, and then, without any to care for me, unattended and uncared for, lay down and die. At times I resolved to take a morsel of food by stealth, (if it could be found,) and make a desperate attempt to escape.

"There were two, however, who seemed not wholly insensible to my condition, these were the wife and daughter of the chief. They manifested a sympathy that had not gathered about me since the first closing in of the night of my captivity upon me. The Indians, at the direction of the chief, began to make preparations to burn the body of my sister. This, it seemed, I could not endure. I sought a place to weep and pray, and I then tasted the blessed ness of realizing that there is One upon whom the heart's heaviest load can be placed, and He never disappointed me. My dark, suicidal thoughts fled, and I became resigned to my lot. Standing by the corpse, with my eyes fastened on that angel–countenaince of Mary Ann, the wife of the chief came to me and gave me to understand that she had by much entreaty, obtained the permission of her lord to give me the privilege of disposing of the dead body as I should choose. This was a great consolation, and I thanked her most earnestly. It lifted a burden from my mind that caused me to weep tears of gratitude, and also to note the finger of that Providence to whom I had fully committed myself, and whom I plainly saw strewing my way with tokens of his kind regards toward me. The chief gave me two blankets, and in these they wrapped the corpse. Orders were then given to two Indians to follow my directions in disposing of the body. I selected a spot in that little garden ground, where I had planted and wept with my dear sister. In this they dug a grave about five feet deep, and into it they gently lowered the remains of my last, my only sister, and closed her last resting–place with the sand. The reader may imagine my feelings, as I stood by that grave. The whole painful past seemed to rush across my mind, as I lingered there. It was the first and only grave in all that valley, and that inclosing my own sister. Around me was a large company of half–dressed, fierce–looking savages, some serious, some mourning, some laughing over this novel method of disposing of the dead; others in breathless silence watched the movements of that dark hour, with a look that seemed to say, 'This is the way white folks do,' and exhibiting no feeling or care beyond that. I longed to plant a rose upon her grave, but the Mohaves knew no beauty, and read no lesson in flowers, and so this mournful pleasure was denied me.

"When the excitement of that hour passed, with it seemed to pass my energy and ambition. I was faint and weak, drowsy and languid. I found but little strength from the scant rations dealt out to me. I was rapidly drooping, and becoming more and more anxious to shut my eyes to all about me, and sink to a sweet, untroubled sleep beneath that green carpeted valley. This was the only time in which, without any reserve, I really longed to die, and cease at once to breathe and suffer. That same woman, the wife of the chief, came again to the solace and relief of my destitution and woe. I was now able to walk but little, and had resigned all care and anxiety, and concluded to wait until those burning sensations caused by want of nourishment should consume the last thread of my life, and shut my eyes and senses in the darkness that now hid them from my sister.

"Just at this time this kind woman came to me with some corn gruel in a hollow stone. I marveled to know how she had obtained it. The handful of seed corn that my sister and I had hid in the ground, between two stones, did not come to my mind. But this woman, this Indian woman, had uncovered a part of what she had deposited against spring planting, had ground it to a coarse meal, and of it prepared this gruel for me. I took it, and soon she brought me more. I began to revive. I felt a new life and strength given me by this morsel, and was cheered by the unlooked–for exhibition of sympathy that attended it. She had the discretion to deny the unnatural cravings that had been kindled by the small quantity she brought first, and dealt a little at a time, until within three days I gained a vigor and cheerfulness I had not felt for weeks. She bestowed this kindness in a sly and unobserved manner, and enjoined secrecy upon me, for a reason which the reader can judge. She had done it when some of her own kin were in a starving condition. It waked up a hope within my bosom that reached beyond the immediate kindness. I could not account for it but by looking to that Power in whose hands are the hearts of the savage as well as the civilized man. I gathered a prospect from these unexpected and kindly interpositions, of an ultimate escape from my bondage. It was the hand of God, and I would do violence to the emotions I then felt and still feel, violence to the strong determination I then made to acknowledge all his benefits, if I should nieglect this opportunity to give a public, grateful record of my sense of his goodness.

"The woman had buried that corn to keep it from the lazy crowd about her, who would have devoured it in a moment, and in utter recklessness of next year's reliance. She did it when deaths by starvation and sickness were occurring every day throughout the settlement.–Had it not been for her, I must have perished. From this circumstance I learned to chide my hasty judgment against ALL the Indian race, and also, that kindness is not always a stranger to the untutored and untamed bosom. I saw in this that their savageness is as much a fruit of their ignorance as of any want of a susceptibility to feel the throbbings of true humanity, if they could be properly appealed to.

" By my own exertions I was able now to procure a little upon which to nourish my half–starved stomach. By using about half of my seed corn, and getting an occasional small dose of bitter, fermented oth–to–toa soup, I managed to drag my life along to March, 1854. During this month and April I procured a few small roots, at a long distance from the village; also some fish from the lake. I took particular pains to guard the little wheat garden that we had planted the autumn before, and I also planted a few kernels of corn and some melon seeds. Day after day I watched this little 'mutautea,' lest the birds might bring upon me another winter like that now passed. In my absence Aespanco would watch it for me. As the fruit of my care and vigilant watching, I gathered about one half bushel of corn, and about the same quantity of wheat. My melons were destroyed.

"During the growing of this crop, I subsisted principally upon a small root,* about the size of a hazel–nut, which I procured by traveling long distances, with fish. Sometimes, after a long and fatiguing search, I would procure a handful of these roots, and, on bringing them to camp, was compelled to divide them with some stout, lazy monsters, who had been sunning themselves all day by the river.

"I also came near losing my corn by the blackbirds. Driven by the same hunger, seemingly, that was preying upon the human tribe, they would fairly darken the air, and it was difficult to keep them off, especially as I was compelled to be absent to get food for immediate use. But they were not the only robbers I had to contend against. There were some who, like our white loafers, had a great horror of honest labor, and they would shun even a little toil, with a conscientious abhorrence, at any hazard. They watched my tittle

* I have several of these ground–nuts now in rny possession.

corn–patch with hungry and thieving eyes, and, but for the chief, would have eaten the corn green and in the ear. As harvest drew near I watched, from before daylight until dark again, to keep off these red vultures and the blackbirds from a spot of ground as large as an ordinary dwelling–house. I had to do my accustomed share of musquite gathering, also, in June and July. This we gathered in abundance. The Colorado overflowed this winter and spring, and the wheat and corn produced well, so that in autumn the tribe was better provided with food than it had been for several years.

"The social habits of these Indians, and the traits of character on which they are founded, and to which they give expression, may be illustrated by a single instance as well as a thousand. The portion of the valley over which the population extends, is about forty miles long. Their convivial seasons were occasions of large gatherings, tumultuous rejoicings, and (so far as their limited productions would allow) of excess in feasting. The year 1854 was one of unusual bounty and thrift. They planted mole than usual; and by labor and the overflow of the river, the seed deposited brought forth an unparalleled increase. During the autumn of that year, the residents of the north part of the valley set apart a day for feasting and merry–making. Notice was given about four weeks beforehand; great preparations were made, and a large number invited. Their supply for the appetite on that day consisted of wheat, corn, pumpkins, beans, etc. These were boiled, and portions of them mixed with ground seed, such as serececa, (seed of a weed,) moeroco, (of pumpkins.) On the day of the feast the Indians masked themselves, some with bark, some with paint, some with skins. On the day previous to the feast, the Indians of our part of the valley, who had been favored with an invitation, were gathered at the house of the chief, preparatory to taking the trip in company to the place of the feast. Some daubed their faces and hair with mud, others with paint, so as to give to each an appearance totally different from his or her natural state. I was told that I could go along with the rest. This to me was no privilege, as I knew too well what cruelty and violence they were capable of when excited, as on their days of public gathering they were liable to be. however, I was safer there than with those whom they left behind.

"The Indians went slowly, sometimes in regular, and sometimes in irregular march, yelling, howling, singing, and gesticulating, until toward night they were wrought up to a perfect phrenzy. They halted about one mile from the "north settlement," and after building a fire, commenced their war–dance, which they kept up until about midnight. On this occasion I witnessed some of the most shameful indecencies, on the part of both male and female, that came to my eye for the five years of my stay among Indians.

"The next morning the Indians who had prepared the feast (some of whom had joined in the dance of the previous evening) came with their squaws, each bearing upon their heads a Coopoesech, containing a cake, or a stone dish filled with soup, or boiled vegetables. Tlhese cakles were made of wheat, ground, and mixed with boiled pumpkins. This dough was rolled out sometimes to two feet in diameter; then placed in hot sand, a leaf and a layer of sand laid over the loaf, and a fire built over the whole, until it was baked through. After depositing these dishes, filled with their prepared dainties, upon a slight mound near by, the whole tribe then joined in a wardance, which lasted nearly twelve hours. After this the dishes and their contents were taken by our party and borne back to our homes, when and where feasting and dancing again commenced, and continued until their supplies were exhausted, and they from sheer weariness were glad to fly to the embrace of sleep. It would be a 'shame even to speak' of all the violence and indecency into which they plunged on these occasions. Suffice it to say that no modesty, no sense of shame, no delicacy, that throw so many wholesome hedges and limitations about the respective sexes on occasions of conviviality where civilization elevates and refines, were there to interfere with scenes the remembrance of which creates a doubt whether these degraded bipeds belong to the human or brute race.

"Thus ended one of the many days of such performances that I witnessed; and I found it difficult to decide whether most of barbarity appeared in these, or at those seasons of wild excitement occasioned by the rousing of their revengeful and brutal passions.

"Of all seasons during my captivity, these of concourse and excitement most disgusted me with the untamed Indian. When I remember what my eyes have witnessed, I am led to wonder and adore at my preservation for a single year, or that my life was not brutalized, a victim to their inhumanity.

"I felt cheerful again, only when that loneliness and desolateness which had haunted me since Difary's death, would sadden and depress my spirits. The sarie woman that had saved my life, and furnished me with ground and seed to raise corn and wheat, and watched it for me for many days, now procured from the chief a place where I might store it, with the promise from him that every kernel should go for my own maintenance."

It is not to go again over the melancholy events that have been rehearsed in the last chapter, that we ask the reader to tarry for a moment ere his eye begins to trace the remaining scenes of Olive's captivity, which furnish the next chapter, and in which we see her under the light of a flickering, unsteady hope of a termination of her captivity either by rescue or death.

But when in haste this chapter was penned for the first edition, it was then, and has since been felt by the writer, that there was an interest hanging about the events of the same, especially upon the closing days and hours of little Mary's brief life, that properly called, according to the intent of this narrative, for a longer stay. A penning of mere facts does not set forth, or glance at all that clusters about that pale, dying child as she lies in the door of the tent, the object of the enchained curious attention of the savages, by whose cold neglect the flower of her sweet life was thus nipped in the bud. And we feel confident of sharing, to some extent, the feelings of the sensitive and intelligent reader, when we state that the two years' suffering, by the pressure of which her life was arrested, and the circumstances surrounding those dying moments, make up a record, than which seldom has there been one that appeals to the tender sensibilities of our being more directly, or to our serious consideration more profitably.

Look at these two girls in the light of the first camp–fire that glowed upon the faces of themselves and their captors, the first dreary evening of their captivity. By one hour's cruel deeds and murder they had suddenly been bereft of parents, brothers, and sisters, and consigned to the complete control of a fiendish set of men, of the cruelty of whose tender mercies they had already received the first and unerring chapter. Look at them toiling day and night, from this on for several periods of twenty–four hours, up rugged ascents, bruised and whipped by the ruggedness of their way and the mercilessness of their lords. Their strength failing; the distance between them and the home and way of the white man increasing; the dreariness and solitude of the region enbosoming them thickening; and each step brooded over by the horrors left behind, and the worse horrors that sat upon the brightest future that at the hlappiest rovings of fancy could be possibly anticipated.

In imagination we lean out our souls to listen to the sobs and sighs that went up from those hearts—hearts bleeding from wounds and pains tenfold more poignant than those that lacerated and wrung their quivering flesh. We look upon them, as with their captors they encircle the wild light of the successive camp–fires, kindled for long distant halts, upon their way to the yet unseen and dreaded home of the "inhabitants of rocks and tents." We look upon them as they are ushered into their new home, greeted with the miost inhuman and terror–kindling reception given them by this unfeeling horde of landsharks; thus to look, imagine, and ponder, we find enough especially when the *age* and *circumstances* of these captive girls are considered, to lash our thoughts with indignation toward their oppressors, and kindle our minds with more than we can express with the word sympalthy for these their innocent victims.

In little less than one year, and into that year is crowded all of toil and suffering that we can credit as possible for them to survive, and then they are sold and again enroute for another new and strange home, in a wild as distant from their Apache home as that from the hill where, but a year before, in their warm flowing blood, their moaning, mangled kindred had been left.

Scarcely had they reached the Mohave Valley ese the elder sister saw with pain, the sad and already apparently irremovable effects of past hardships upon the constitution of the younger. What tenderness, what caution, what vigilant watching, what anxious, unrelieved solicitude mark the conduct of that noble heart toward her declining and only sister? Indeed, what interest prompted her to do all in her power to preserve her life? Not only her only sister, but the only one (to her then) that remained of the family from whom they had been ruthlessly torn. And should her lamp of life cease, thereby would be extinguished the last earthly solace and cordial for the dark prison life that inclosed her, and that threw its wells of gloom and adamant between her and the abodes and sunshine of civilized life. Yet death had marked that little cherub girl for an early victim. Slowly, and yet uncomplainingly, does her feeble frame and strength yield to the heavy hand of woe and want that met her, in all the ghastliness and horror of unchangeable doom, at every turn and hour of her weary days. What mystery hangs upon events and persons! How impenetrable the permissions of Providence! How impalpable and evasive of all our wisdom that secret power, by which cherished plans and purposes are often shaped to conclusions and terminations so wide of the bright design that lighted them on to happy accomnplishment in the mind of the mortal proposer!

Mary Ann had been the fondly cherished, and teinderly nursed idol of that domestic group. Early had she exhibited a precocity in intellect, and in moral sensitiveness and attainment, that had made her the subject of a peculiar parental affection, and the ever cheerful radiating center of light, and love, and happiness to the remainder of the juvenile family. But she ever possessed a strength of body and vigor of health far inferior, and disproportioned to her mental and moral progress. She was a correct reader at four years. She was kept almost constantly at school, both from her choice, and the promise she gave to delighted parents of a future appreciation and good improvement of these advantages. With the early exhibition of an earnest thirst for knowledge that she gave, there was also a strict regard for truth, and a hearty, happy obedience to the law of God and the authority of her parents. At five years and a half she had read her Bible through. She was a constant attendant upon Sabbath school, into all the exercises of which she entered with delight; and to her rapid improvement and profit in the subjects with which she there became intimate and identified, may be attributed the moral superiority she displayed during her captivity.

She had a clear, sweet voice, and the children now live in this state who have witnessed the earnestness and rapture with which she joined in singing the hymns allotted to Sabbath–school hours. O how little of the sad after–part of Mary's life entered into the minds of those parents as thus they directed the childish, tempted steps of their little daughter into the paths of religious pursuits and obedience.

Who shall say that the facts in her childish experience and years herein glanced at, had not essentially to do with the spirit and preparedness that she brought to the encountering and enduring of the terrible fate that closed her eyes among savages at eight years of age.

As we look at her fading, withering, and wasting at the touch of cold cruelty, the object of anxious watchings and frequent and severe painstaking on the part of her elder sister, who spared no labor or fatigue to glean the saving morsel to prolong her sinking life, we can but adore that never–sleeping Goodness that had strewn her way to this dark scene with so many preparing influences and counsels.

Young as she was, she with her sister were first to voice those hymns of praise to the one God, in which the grateful offerings of Christian hearts go up to him, in the ear of an untutored and demoralized tribe of savages. Hers was the first Christian death they ever witnessed, perhaps the last; and upon her, as with composure and cheerfulness (not the sullen submission of which they boast) she came down to the vale of death, they gazed with every indication of an interest and curiosity that showed the workings of something more than the ordinary solemnities that had gathered them about the paling cheek and quivering lip of members of their own tribe.

Precious girl! sweet flower! nipped in the bud by untimely and rude blasts. Yet the fragrance of the ripe virtues that budded and blossomed upon so tender and frail a stalk shall not die. If ever the bright throng that flame near the throne would delight to cease their song, descend and poise on steady wing to wait the last heaving of a suffering, mortal's bosom, that at the parting breath they might encircle the fluttering spirit and bear it to the bosom of God, it was when thou didst, upon the breath of sacred song, joined in by thy living sister, yield thy spirit to Him who kindly cut short thy sufferings that he might begin thy bliss.

A Sabbath–school scholar, dying in an Indian camp, three hundred miles from even the nearest trail of the white man, buoyed and gladdened by bright visions of beatitudes that make her oblivious of present pain, and long to enter upon the future estate to which a correct and earnest instruction had been pointing!

Who can say but that there lives the little Mohave boy or girl, or the youth who will yet live to rehearse in the ear of a listening American auditory, and in a rough, uncouth jargon, the wondrous impression of that hour upon his mind.

Already we see the arms of civilization embracing a small remnant of that waning tribe, and among its revived records, though unwritten, we find the death of the American captive in the door of the chief's "Pasioao." When they gathered about her at that dying moment, many were the curious questions with which some of them sought to ascertain the secret of her (to them) strange appearance. The sacred hymns learned in Sabbath school and at a domestic shrine, and upon which that little spirit now breathed its devout emotions in the ear of God, were inquired after. They asked her where she expected to go?

She told them that she was going to a better place than the mound to which they sent the spirits of their dead. And many questions did they ask her and her older sister as to the extent of the knowledge they had of such a bright world, if one there was. And though replies to many of their queries before had been met by mockings and ridicule, yet now not one gazed, or listened, or questioned, to manifest any disposition to taunt or accuse at the hour of that strange dying. The wife of the chief plied her questions with earnestness, and with an air of sincerity, and the exhibition of the most intense mental agitation, showing that she was not wholly incredulous of the new and strange replies she received.

TALE OF THE TWO CAPTIVES

One night a large company were assembled at the hut of one of the sub–chiefs. It was said that this Indian, Adpadarama, was the illegitimate son of the present chief, and there was considerable dispute between him and two of the chief's legitimate sons as to their respective rights to the chiefship on the death of the father.

At the gathering referred to the following anecdote was related, which is here given to show the strength of their superstitions, and the unmitigated cruelties which are sometimes perpetrated by them under the sanction of these barbaric beliefs. This sub–chief said that one day, when he, in company with several of his relatives and two Cochopa captives, was away in the mountains on a hunting–tour, his (reputed) father fell violently sick. He grew worse for several days. One day he was thought to be dying. "When I was convinced that he could not live," said Adpadarama, or to that effect, "I resolved to kill one of the captives, and then wait until my father should die, when I would kill the other. So I took a stone tomahawk and went out to the little fire near the camping–tent, where they were eating some berries they had just picked, and I told one of them to step out, for I was a going to kill her to see if it would not save my father. Then she cried," (and at this he showed by signs, and frowns, and all manner of gestures how delighted he was at her misery,) " and begged for her life. But I went up to her and struck her twice with this tomahawk, when she fell dead upon the ground. I then told the other that I should kill her so soon as my father died; that I should burn them both with his body, and then they would go to be his slaves up in yonder eliercha," (pointing to their heavenly hill.) "Well, about two days after my father died, and I was mad to think that the killing of the captive had not saved him. So I went straight and killed the other, but I killed her by burning, so as to be sure that the flames should take her to my father to serve him forever."

Such are facts that dimly hint at the vague and atrocious theories that crowd their brain and hold iron sway over their minds. And in all the abominations and indecencies authorized by their superstitions, they are not only prompt and faithful, but the more degrading and barbarous the rite, the more does their zeal and enthusiasm kindle at its performance.

Adpadarama said he burned, as soon as he returned, his father's house, and all his dishes, and utensils, and bark–garments, so that his father might have them to contribute to his happiness where he had gone.

CHAPTER V

The Mohaves–Their Sports–An Expedition of Hostility against the Cochopas–Its Design–Tradition concerning it–The Preparation–Their Custom of Sacrificing a Prisoner on the Death in War of One of their own Number–The Anxiety of Olive–They depart–Their Return–The Fruit of the Expedition–The Five Cochopa Captives Nowereha–Her Attempt to Escape–Her Recapture and Horrid Death–The Physicians–Evil Spirits–The Mohave Mode of Doctoring–The Yumnas–"Francisco," the Yuma Indian–Hopes of Escape.

"In the spring of 1854, the project of some exciting hostile expedition against a distant tribe was agitated among the Mohaves. It was some time before any but the 'Council' knew of the definite purpose of the expedition. But when their plans had been laid, and all their intentions circulated among the tribe, it proved to be one of war upon the Cochopas, a large tribe seven hundred miles away. The Cochopas were a tribe with whom the Mohlaves had never been at peace. According to tradition, this hostility had been kept actively flaming through all past generations. And the Mohaves were relying with equal certainty upon the truth of traditional prophecy that they were ultimately to subject the Cochopas to their sway, or obliterate them. The Mohaves had as yet been successful in every engagement. They were confident of success, and this was all the glory their ambition was capable of grasping. As for any intrinsic merit in the matter of the contest, none was known to exist. About sixty warriors made preparations for a long time to undertake the expedition.

"Bows and arrows and war–clubs were prepared in abundance, also stone–knives. The war–club was made of a very solid wood that grew upon the mountain. It was of a tree that they called 'Cooachee,' very hard and heavy, and lost but very little of its weight in the seasoning process.

"Great preparations were also made by the squaws, though with much reluctance, as most of them were opposed to the expedition, as they had been also in the past to kindred ones. Those of them; who had husbands and brothers enlisted in the expedition, tried every expedient in their power to dissuade them from it. They accused them of folly and a mere lust of war, and prayed them not thus to expose their own lives and the lives of their dependent ones. It was reported that since the last attack upon them, the Cochopees had strengthened themselves with numerous and powerful allies, by uniting several surrounding tribes with themselves for purposes of war. This was pleaded by these interested women against the present purpose, as they feared that this distant tribe would be now able to avenge past injury, besides beating the Mohaves in this projected engagement. But go they would, and on the day of their departure there was a convocation of nearly the whole tribe, and it was a time of wild, savage excitement and deep mourning.

"I soon learned, though by mere accident, that far as life was concerned, I had an interest in this expedition equal to that of the most exposed among the warriors. It had been an unvarying custom among them that if any of their number should be slain in battle, the lives of prisoners or captives must be sacrificed therefor, up to the number of the slain, (if that nunber should be among them,) and that in the most torturing manner. This was not done to appease their gods, for they had none, but was a gift to the spirits of the other spheres. Their only theory about a Supreme Being is that there is a chief of all the Indians who reigns in splendor and pomp, and that his reign is one of wisdom and equity, and would last forever. They believed that at the gate of their elysium a porter was in constant attendance, who received all good, brave Indians, and welcomed them to immense hunting–grounds and all manner of sensual pleasures; that if one sought admittance there without a bow and hunting implements, he was to subsist as best he could, for no provision was to be made for him after leaving his tribe. Many were the questions they asked me after they had ascertained what I believed concerning the nature of the heaven of which I spoke, and the employments there. But generally they would wind up the conversation with ridicule and mockings. When they saw me weep or in trouble they would sometimes say: 'Why don't you look up and call your great God out of the sky, and have him take you up there.' But under all this I could plainly see that their questions were not wholly insincere. They frequently marveled, and occasionally one would say: 'You whites are a singular people; I should like to know what you will be when a great many moons have gone by?' Sometimes they would say as did the Apaches, that we must be fools for believing that heaven was above the sky; that if it were so the people would drop down. One of the squaws said tauntingly to me: 'When you go to your heaven you had better take a strong piece of bark and tie yourself up, or you will be coming down among us again.' After the soldiers had departed they told me plainly that my life must pay for the first one that might be slain during this contest.

"I had but a little before learned that we were not much further from the white settlements than when among the Apaches, and had been fondly hoping that as parties of the tribe occasionally made excursions to the settlements, I might yet make my situation known and obtain relief. But now I was shut up to the alternatives of either making an immediate effort to escape, which would be sure to cost my life if detected, or to wait in dreadful suspense the bare probability of none of these soldiers being slain, as the only chance for myself if I remained.

"The report of the strengthening of the Cochopas since their last expedition gave me reason to fear the worst. Thus for a long time, and just after having reached a bright place (if such there can be in such a situation) in my captivity, I was thrown into the gloomiest apprehensions for my life. I could not calculate upon life; I did not.

"For five months not a night did I close my eyes for a troubled sleep, or wake in the morning but last and first were the thoughts of the slender thread upon which my life was hung. The faint prospect in which I had been indulging, that their plans of increasing traffic with the Mexicans and whites might open the doors for my return, was now nearly blasted.

"I had been out one fine day in August several miles gathering roots for the chief's family, and returning a little before sunset, as I came in sight of the village I saw an Indian at some distance beyond the town descending a hill to the river from the other side. He was so far away that it was impossible for me to tell whether he was a Yuma or a Mohave. These two tribes were on friendly terms, and frequent 'criers' or news–carriers passed between them. I thought at once of the absent warriors, and of my vital interest in the success or failure of their causeless, barbarous crusade. I soon saw that he was a Mohave, and tremblingly believed that I could mark him as one of the army.

"With trembling and fear I watch his hastened though evidently wearied pace. He went down into the river and as he rose again upon the bank I recognized him. 'He is wearied,' I said, 'and jogs heavily along as though he had become nearly exhausted from long travel. Why can he be coming in alone?' Questions of this character played across my mind, and were asked aloud by me ere I was aware, each like a pointed javelin lashing and tormenting my fears. 'Have the rest all perished?' again I exclaimed;'at any rate the decisive hour has come with me.'

"I stopped; my approach to the village had not been observed. I resolved to wait and seek to cover one desperate effort to escape under the first shades of night. I threw myself flat upon the ground; I looked in every direction; mountain chains were strung around me on every side like bulwarks of adamant, and if trails led through them I knew them not. I partly raised myself up. I saw that Indian turn into a hut upon the outskirts of the town. In a few moments the 'criers' were out and bounding to the river and to the foot hills. Each on his way started others, and soon the news was flying as on telegraphic wires. *'But what new*?' I could but exclaim. I started up and resolved to hasten to our hut and wait in silence the full returns.

"I could imagine that I saw my doom written in the countenance of every Mohave I met. But each one maintained a surly reserve or turned upon me a sarcastic smile. A crowd was gathering fast, but not one word was let fall for my ear. In total, awful silence I looked, I watched, I guessed, but dared not speak. It seemed that every one was reading and playing with my agitation.

Soon the assemblage was convenied, a fire was lighted, and'Ohitia' rose up to speak; I listened, and my heart seemed to leap to my mouth as he proceeded to state, in substance, thus: 'Mohaves have triumphed; five prisoners taken; all on their way; none of our men killed; they will be in to–morrow!'

"Again one of the blackest clouds that darkened the sky of my Mohave captivity broke, and the sunshine of gladness and gratitude was upon my heart. Tears of gratitude ran freely down my face. I buried my face in my hands and silently thanked God. I sought a place alone, where I might give fulll vent to my feelings of thanksgiving to my heavenly Father. I saw his goodness, in whose hands are the reins of the wildest battle storm, and thanked him that this expedition, so freighted with anxiety, had issued so mercifully to me.

"The next day four more came in with the captives, and in a few days all were returned, without even a scar to tell of the danger they had passed. The next day after the coming of the last party, a meeting of the whole tribe was called, and one of the most enthusiastic rejoicing seasons I ever witnessed among them it was. It lasted, indeed, for several days. They danced, sung, shouted, and played their cornstalk flutes until for very weariness they were compelled to refrain. It was their custom never to eat salted meat for the next moon after the coming of a captive among them. Hence our salt fish were for several days left to an undisturbed repose.

"Among the captives they had stolen from the unoffending Cochopas, and brought in with them, was a handsome, fair complexioned young woman, of about twenty–five years of age. She was as beautiful an Indian woman as I have ever seen; tall, graceful, and ladylike in her appearance. She had a fairer, lighter skin than the Mohaves or the other Cochopa captives. But I saw upon her countenance and in her eyes the traces of an awful grief. The rest of the captives appeared well and indifferent about themselves.

"This woman called herself 'Nowereha.' Her language was as foreign to the Mohaves as the American, except to the few soldiers that had been among them. The other captives were girls from twelve to sixteen years old; and while they seemed to wear a 'don't care' appearance, this Nowereha was perfectly bowed down with grief. I observed she tasted but little food. She kept up a constant moaning and wailing, except when checked by the threats of her boastful captors. I became very much interested in her, and sought to learn the circumstances under which she had been torn from her home. Of her grief I thought I know something. She tried to converse with me.

"With much difficulty I learned of her what had happened since the going of the Mohave warriors among her tribe, and this fully explained her extreme melancholy. Their town was attacked in the night by the Mohave warriors, and after a short engagement the Cochopas were put to flight; the Mohaves hotly pursued them. Nowereha had a child about two months old; but after running a short distance her husband came up with her, grasped the child, and run on before This was an act showing a humaneness that a Mohave warrior did not possess, for he would have compelled his wife to carry the child, he kicking her along before him. She was overtaken and captured.

"For one week Nowereha wandered about the village by day, a perfect image of desperation and despair. At times she seemed insane: she slept but little at night. The thieving, cruel Mohaves who had taken her, and were making merry over her griefs, knew full well the cause of it all. They knew that without provocation they had robbed her of her child, and her child of its mother. They knew the attraction drawing her back to her tribe, and they watched her closely. But no interest or concern did they manifest save to mock and torment her.

"Early one morning it was noised through the village that Nowereha was missing. I had observed her the day before, when the chief's daughter gave her some corn, to take part of the same, after grind ing the rest, to make a cake and hide it in her dress. When these captives were brought in, they were assigned different places through the valley at which to stop. Search was made to see if she had not sought the abiding–place of some of her fellow captives. This caused some delay, which I was glad to see, though I dared not express my true feelings.

"When it was ascertained that she had probably undertaken to return, every path and every space dividing the immediate trails was searched, to find if possible some trace to guide a band of pursuers. A large number were stationed in different parts of the valley, and the most vigilant watch was kept during the night, while others started in quest of her upon the way they supposed she had taken to go back. When I saw a day and night pass in these fruitless attempts, I began to hope for the safety of the fuigitive. I had seen enough of her to know that she was resolved and of unconquerable determination. Some conjectured that she had been betrayed away; others that she had drowned herself, and others that she had taken to the river and swam away. They finally concluded that she had killed herself, and gave up the search, vowing that if she had fled they would yet have her and be avenged.

"Just before night, several days after this, a Yuma Indian came suddenly into camp, driving this Cochopa captive. She was the most distressed–looking being imaginable when she returned. Hier hair disheveled, her few old clothes torn, (they were woolen clothes,) her eyes swollen, and every feature of her noble countenance distorted.

"'Criers' were kept constantly on the way between the Mohaves and Yumas, bearing news from tribe to tribe. These messengers were their newscarriers and sentinels. Frequently two criers were employed, (sometimes more,) one from each tribe. These would have their meeting–stations. At these stations these criers would meet with promptness, and by word of mouth each would deposit his store of news with his fellow–expressman, and then each would return to his own tribe with the news. When the news was important, or was of a warning character, as in time of war, they would not wait for the fleet foot of the 'runner,' but had their signal fires well understood, which would telegraph the news hundreds of miles in a few hours. One of these Yuma criers, about four days after the disappearance of Nowereha, was coming to his station on the road connecting these two tribes, when he spied a woman under a shelf of the rock on the opposite side of the river. Ie immediately plunged into the stream and went to her. He knew the tribe to which she belonged, and that the Mohaves had been making war upon them. TIe immediately started back with her to the Mohave village. It was a law to which they punctually lived, to return all fleeing fugitives or captives of a firiendly tribe.

"It seemed that she had concealed that portion of the corn meal she did not bake, with a view of undertaking to escape.

"When she went out that night she plunged immediately into the river to prevent them from tracking her. She swam several miles that night, and then hid herself in a willow wood; thinking that they would be in close pursuit, she resolved to remain there until they should give iup hunting for her. Here she remained nearly two days, and her pursueis were very near her several times. She then started, and swam where the river was not too rapid and shallow, when she would out and bound over the rocks. In this way, traveling only in the night, slhe had gone near one hundred and thirty miles. She was, as she supposed, safely hid in a cave, waiting, the return of night, when the Yuma found her.

"'On her return another noisy meeting was called, and they spent the night in one of their victory dances. They would dance around her, shout in lier ears, spit in her face, and show their threats of a murderous design, assuring her that they would soon have her where she would give them no more trouble by running away.

"The next morning a post was firmly placed in the ground, and about eight feet fiom thc ground a cross–beam was attached. They then drove large, rough wooden spikes through the palms of poor Nowereha's hands, and by these they lifted her to the cross and drove the spikes into the soft wood of the beam, extending her hands as far as they could. They then, with pieces of bark stuck with thorns, tied her head firmly back to the upright post, drove spikes through her ankles, and for a time left her in this condition.

"They soon returned, and placing me with their Cochopa captives neai the sufferer, bid us keep our eyes upon her until she died. This they did, as they afterward said, to exhibit to me what I might expect if they should catch me attempting to escape. They then comlnmenced running round Nowerehla in regular circles, hallooing, stamping, and taunting like so many demons, in the most wild and frenzied manner. After a little while several of them supplied themselves with bows and arrows, and at every circlet would hurl one of these poisoned instruments of death into her quivering flesh. Occasionally she would cry aloud, and in the most pitiful manner. This awakened from that mocking, heartless crowd the most deafening yells.

HORRID DEATH OF THE INDIAN CAPTIVE

"She hung in this dreadful condition for over two hours ere I was certain she was dead, all the while bleeding and sighing, her body mangled in the most shocking mananer. When she would cry aloud they–would stuff rags in her mouth, and thus silence her. Wlien tlhey were quite sure she was dead, and that they could no longer inflict pain upon her, they took her body to a funerial pile and burned it.

"I had before this thought, since I had come to know of tie vicinity of the whites, that I would get some knowledge of the way to their abodes by means of the occasional visits the Molaves made to them, and make my escape. But this scene discouraged me, however, and each day I found myself, not witltout hope it is true, but settling down into such contentment as I could with my lot. For the next eighteen months during which I was witness to their conduct, these Mohaves took more care and exercised more forethought in the matter of their food. They did not suffer, and seemed to determine not to suffer the return of a season like 1852.

"I saw but little reason to expect anythin(g else than the spending of my years among them, and I had no anxiety that they should be many. I saw around me none butt savages, and (dreadfil as was the thought) among whom I must spend my days. There were some with vlwhom I had become intimately acquainted, and fiom whom I had received humane and friendly treatment, exhibiting real kindness. I thought it best now to conciliate the best wishes of all, and by every possible means to avoid all occasions of awakening their displeasure, or enkindling their unrepentant, noncontrollable temper and passions.

"There were some few for whom I began.to feel a degree of attachment. Every spot in that valley that had any attraction, or offered a retreat to the sorrowing soul, had become familiar, and upon mnlch of its adjacent scenery I delighted to gaze. Every day had its mnonotony of toil, and thus I plodded on.

"To escape seemed impossible, and to make an unsuccessful attempt would be worse than death. Friends or kindred to look after or care for me, I had none, as I then supposed. I thought it best to re ceive my daily allotment with submission, and not darken it with a borrowed trouble; to merit and covet the good–will of my captors, wethier I received it or not. At times the past, with all its checkered scenes, would roll up before me, but all of it that was most deeply engraven upon my mind was that which I would be soonest to forget if I could. Time seemed to take a more rapid flight; I hardly could wake up to the reality of so long, a captivity among savages, and really imagined myself happy for short periods.

"I considered my age, mny sex, my exposure, and was again in trouble, though to the honori of these savages let it be said, they never offered the least unchaste abuse to me.

"During the summer of 1855 I was eye–witness to another illustration of their superstition, and of its implacability when appealed to. The Moliaves had but a simple system or theory of medicine. They divide disease into spiritual and physical, or at least they used terms that conveyed such an impression as this to my mind. The latter they treated mainly to an application of their medical leaf, generally sweatinig the patient by wrapping him in blankets and placing him over the steam from these leaves warmed in water. For the treatment of their spiritual or more malignant discases they have physicians. All diseases were ranked under the latter class that had baffled the virtue of the medical leaf, and that were considered dangerous.

"In the summer of 1855 a sickness prevailed to a considerable extent, very much resembling in its workings the more malignant fevers. Several died. Members of the families of two of the sub–chiefs were sick, and their physicians were called. These 'M.D.s' were above the need of pills, and plasters, and powders, and performed their cures by manipulations, and all manner of contortions of their own bodies, which were performed with loud weeping and wailing of the most extravagant kind over the sick. They professed to be in league and intimacy with the spirits of the departed, and from whose superior knowledge and position they were guided in all their curative processes. Two of these were called to the sick bedside of the children of these chiefs. They wailed and wrung their hands, and twisted themselves into all manner of shapes over them for some time, but it was in vain, the patients died. They had lost several patients lately, and already their medical repute was low in the market. Threats had already followed them from house to house, as their failures were known. After the death of these children of rank, vengeance was sworn upon them, as they were accused of having bargained themselves to the evil spirits for purpose of injury to the tribe. They knew of their danger and hid themselves on the other side of the river. For several days search was made, but in vain. They had relatives and friends who kept constant guard over them. But such was the feeling created by the complainings of those who had lost children and friends by their alleged conspiracy with devils, that the tribe demanded their lives, and the chief gave orders for their arrest. But their friends managed in a sly way to conceal them for some ti no, though they did not dare to let their manager. be known to the rest of the tribe. They were found, alrested, and burned alive.

"The Mohaves believe that when their friends die they depart to a certain high hill in the western section of their territory. That they there pursue their avocation free from the ills and pains of their present life, if they had been good and brave. But they held that all cowardly Indians (and bravery was the good with them) were tormented with hardships and failures, sickness and defeats. This hill or hades, they never dared visit. It was thronged with thousands who were ready to wreak vengeance upon the mortal who dared intrude upon this sacred ground.

'Up to the middle of February, 1856, nothing occuiired connected with my allotment that would be of interest to the reader. One day as I was grinding musquite near the door of our dwelling, a lad came running up to me in haste, and said that Fran cisco, a Yuma crier, was on his way to the Mohaves, and that lie was coming to try and get me away to the whites. The report created a momentary strange sensation, but I thought it probably was a rumor gotten up by these idlers (as they were wont to do) merely to deceive and excite me to their own gratification. In a few moments, however, the report was circulating on good authority, and as a reality. One of the sub–chiefs came in said that a Yuma Indian, named Francisco, was now on his way with positive orders for my immediate release and safe return to the fort.

"I knew that there were white persons at Fort Yuma, but did not know my distance from the place. I knew, too, that intercourse of some kind was constantly kept up with the Yumas and the tribes extending that way, and thought that they had perhaps gained traces of my situation by this means. But as yet I had nothing definite upon which to place confidence.

"I saw in a few hours that full credit was given to the report by the Mohaves, for a sudden commotion was created, and it was enkindling excitement throughout the settlement. The report spread over the valley with astonishing speed, by means of their criers, and a crowd was gathering, and the chliefs and principal men were summoned to a council by their head 'Aespaniola,' with whom I stayed. Aespani'ola was a tall, strongly built man, active and generally happy. He seemed to possess a mildness of dispo sition and to maintain a gravity and seriousness in deportment that was rare among them. He ruled a council (noisy as they sometimes were) with an ease and authority such as but few Indians can command, if the Mohaves be a fair example. This council presented the appearance of an aimless convening of wild maniacs, more than that of men, met to deliberate. I looked upon the scene as a silent but narrowly watched spectator, but was not permitted to be in the crowd or to hear what was said.

"I knew the declared object of the gathering, and was the subject of most anxious thoughts as to its issue and results. I thought I saw upon the part of some of them, a designed working of themselves into a mad phrenzy, as if preparatory to some brutal deed. I queried whether yet the report was not false; and also as to the persons who had sent the reported message, and by whom it might be conveyed. I tried to detect the prevailing feeling among the most influential of the council, but could not. Sometimes I doubted whether all this excitement could have been gotten up on the mere question of my return to the whites.

"For some time past they had manifested but little watchfulness, care, or concern about me. But still, though I was debarred from the council, I had heard enough to know that it was only about me and the reported demand for my liberty.

"In the midst of the uproar and confusion the approach of Francisco was announced. The debate suddenly ceased, and it was a matter of much interest to mre to be able to mark, as I did, the various manifestations by which different ones received him.

"Some were sullen, and would hardly treat him with any cordiality; others were indifferent, and with a shakle of the head would say, 'Degee, degee, ontoa, ontoa,' (I don't care for the captive;) others were angry, and advised that he be kept out of the council and driven back at once; others were dignified and serious.

"I saw Francisco enter the council, and I was at once seized by two Indians and bade be off to another part of the village. I found myself shut up alone, unattended, unprotected. A message as fromn a land of light had suddenly broken in upon my dark situation, and over it, and also over my destiny; the most intense excitement was prevailing, more vehemenrt, if possible, than any before, and I denied the privilege of a plea or a word to turn the scale in favor of my rights, my yearnings, my hopes, or my prayers.

"I did pray God then to rule that council. My life was again hung up as upon a single hair. The most of my dread for the present was, that these savages of untamed passions would become excited against my release, and enraged that the place of my abode had been found out. I feared and trembled for my fate, and could not sleep. For three days and most of three nights this Iloisy council continued; at times the disputants became angriy (as Francisco afterward told me) as rival opinions and resolutions fired their breasts. As yet I knew not by what means my locality had becomne known, or who had sent the demand; nor did I know as yet that anything more than a word of mouth message had been sent."

CHAPTER VI

Lorenzo Oatman–His Stay at Fort Yuma–Goes with Dr. Hewit to San Francisco–His constant Misery on Account of his Sisters–Dark Thoughts–Cold Sympathy–Goes to the Mines–Resolves to go to Los Angeles to learn if possible of his Sisters–His earnest but fruit less Endeavors–The Lesson–Report brought by Mr. Roulit of two Captives among the Mohaves–The false Report of Mr. Black–Mr. Grinell–Petitions the Governor–Petitions Congress–The Report of the Rescue of Olive–Mr. Low.

We now ask the reader to trace with us for a few pages, a brief account of the mnovemnents and efforts (mainly by her brother) by which this scene had been waked up in the captive home of Miss Olive, and that had extended this new opening for her rescue. In chapter third we left Lorenzo disabled, but slowly recovering from the effect of his bruises, at Fort Yuma. Of the kindness of Dr. Hewit we there spoke.

We here give a narrative of the winding, carethorned course of the boy of scarce fifteen years, for the next five years, and the ceaseless toil and vigilance he exercised to restore those captive sisters; as we have received the items from his own mouth. It is worth the painstaking that its perusal wvill cost, showing as it does, a true affection and regard for his kindred, while the discretion and perseverance by which his promptings were guided would do honor to the man of thirty.

He was at Fort Yuma three months, or nearly that time. Dr. Hewit continued to watch over him up to San Francisco, and until Ie went East, and then provided for him a home. Besides, lie did all in his power to aid him in ascertaining some traces of his sisters. At the fort Lorenzo knew that his sisters were captives. He entreated Commander Heinsalman, as well as did others. to make some effort to regain them, but it was vain that hle tius pleaded for help. The officers and force at the fort were awake to the reasonableness and justice of his plea. Some of them anxiously longed to make a thorough search for them. They were not permitted to carry the exposed family bread and needed defense, but had been out and seen the spot where they had met a cruel death, and now they longed to follow the savage Apache to his hliding–place, break the arm of the oppressor, and if possible, rescue the living spoil they had taken. The short time of absence granted to Lieutenant Maury and Captain Davis, though well filled up and faithfully, could not reach the distant captives.

At times this brother resolved to arm himself, and take a pack of provisions and start, either to accomplish their rescue or die with them. But this step would have only proved a short road to one of their funeral piles. In June of this year the entire force was removed from the fort to San Diego, except about a dozen men to guard the ferrymen. On the 26th of June, with Dr. Hlewit, Lorenzo came to San Francisco. After Dr. Hewit had left for the States he began to reflect on his loneliness, and more deeply than ever upon his condition and that of his sisters. Sometimes he would stray upon the hills at night in the rear of the city, so racked with despair and grief as to determine upon taking his own life, if hle could not secure the rescue of the captives. He found the stirring, throbbing life of San Francisco beating almost exclusively to the impulses of gold–lunting. Of acquaintances he had none, nor did he possess any desire to make them.

"Often," he says, " have I strolled out upon these sidewalks and traveled on until I was among the hills to which these streets conducted me, to the late hour of the night, stung by thinking and reflecting upon the past and present of our family kingdom." He was given employment by the firm in whose care he had been left by Dr. Hewit. He soon found that tasks were assigned him in the wholesale establish–meut beyond his years and strength. He seriously injured himiself by lifting, and was compelled to leave. "This I regretted," he says, "for I found non–employment a misery."

Every hour his mind was still hlaunted by the *one all-absorbing theme!* His sisters, his own dear sisters, spirit of his spirit, and blood of his blood, were in captivity. For aught he knew, they were suffering cruelties and abuse worse than death itself, at the hands of their captors. He could not engage steadily in any employment. Dark and distressing thoughts were continually following him. No wonder that he would often break out with utterances like these: "O my God! must they there remain? Can there be no method devised to rescue them? Are they still alive, or have they suffered a cruel death? I will know if I live."

He had no disposition to make acquaintances, unless to obtain sympathy and help for the one attempt that from the first he had meditated; no temptation to plunge into vice to drown his trouble, for he only lived to see them rescued, if yet alive.

Thus three years passed away, some of the time in the mines and a portion of it in the city. Frequently his sadness was noticed, and its cause kindly inquired after, upon which hlie would give an outline of the circumstances that had led to his present uncheered condition. Sonme would weep and manifest much anxiety to do something to aid him in the recovery of his lost kindred; others would wonder and say nothing; others–*strangers!*–were sometimes incredulous, and scoffed. He knew that the route by which he had reached this country was still traveled by emigiants, andl hlie resolved upon going to Los

Angeles with the hope that he might there obtain some knowledge of the state of things in the region of Fort Yuma. Accordingly, in October of 1854, he started for that place, and resolved there to stay until he might obtain some traces of his sisters, if it should take a whole lifetime. He found there those who had lately passed over the road, and some who had spent a short time at the stopping–places so sadly familiar to him. He inquired, and wrote letters, and used all diligence (as some persons now in that region, and others in San Francisco can bear witness) to accomplish the one end of all his care. He worked by the month a part of the time to earn a living, and spent the remainder in devising and setting on foot means to explore the region lying about Fort Yuma and beyond. Thus, in the most miserable state of mind, and in utter fruitlessness of endeavor, passed away almost a year. During the spring of 1855 several emigrants came by this trail. Of them he could learn nothing,. only that they had heard at Fort Yuma of the fate of the "family of Oatrmans."

One company there was who told him of a 3Ir. (Grinell, a carpenter at Fort Yuma, who had told that he kinew of the massacre of the Oatman family, and of the captivity of the girls, and that like intended to do all in his power to recover them. He said that their brother, who was left for dead, was now alive, and at Los Angeles; that a letter had been received at the fort from him concerning his sisters, and that he should exert himself to find them out and rescue them. This Mr. Grinell also stated that he had come to Fort Yuma in 1853, and had been making inquiries of the Yumas ever since concerning these captive girls. Beyond this, no ray of light broke upon the thickening gloom of that despairing brother. He tried to raise companions to attend him in the pursuit of them to the mountains. At one time names were registered, and all preparations made by a large company of volunteers, who were going out for this purpose, but a trivial circumstance broke up the anticipated expedition and frustrated the whole plan. And at other times other kindred plans were laid, and well–nigh matured, but some unforeseen occasion for postponement or abandonment would suddenly come up. He found friends, and friends to the cherished ambition of his heart, in whom flowed the currents of a true and positive sympathy, and who were ready to peril life in assisting him in the consummation of his life–object. And often he found this concealed under the roughest garb, while sometimes smooth words and a polished exterior proffered no means of help beyond mere appearance.

He says: "I learned, amid the harassings of that year two things: 1. That men did not come across the plains to hunt captives among the Indians; 2. That a true sympathy is oftenest found among those who have themselves also suffered." He found that to engage an ally in an undertaking dictated by pity for suffering friends, one must go among those who have felt the pang of kindred ills. Often, when he thought all was ready to start with an engaged party to scour the Apache country, did he find some trifling excuse called in to cover a retreat from an undertaking with which these subjects of a "show sympathy" had no *real* interest from the first. Thus he came to learn human nature, but was not discouraged. Could we turn upon these pages the full tide of the heart–yearnings and questionings that struggled in that young man's heart, by daylight, by twilight, by moonlight, as he strolled (as often he did) for reflection upon old ocean's shore, on the sandy beach, in the wood, it might cause the heart of the reader to give heed to the tales of true grief that daily strew his way, and kindle a just contempt for a *mere artificial sympathy.*

The year 1855 found him undaunted, still pressing on to the dictates of *duty to his beloved sisters*. Every failure and mishap but kindled his zeal anew. Parties of men organized late in 1855 to hunt gold on the Mohave River, about one hundred miles from San Bernardino. He joined several of these, with the promise from men among them that they would turn their excursion into a hunt for his kindred. Once he succeeded in getting as far as, and even beyond (though further north) Fort Yuma. But still he could not prevail upon a sufficient number to go as far as the Apache country to make it safe to venture. Miany would say that his sisters were dead, and it was useless to hunt them. He joined surveying parties with this same one object in view. In 1855 a force equal to the one that was there in 1851 was again at Fort Yuma, and several of the same officers andmen. The place of Commander Hein salman had been filled by another man. In December, 1855, a party of five men resolved to join Mr. Oatman and search for his sisters until some definite knowledge of them might be obtained. They spent several weeks south and west of Fort Yuma, and had returned to San Bernardino to re–supply themselves with provisions for a trip further north.

While at this place Lorenzo received a letter from a friend residing at the Monte, and stating that a Mr. Rowlit had just come in across the plains; that he spent some time at Fort Yuma, and there learned from the officers that, through the Yuma Indians, Mr. Grinell had gathered intimations of the fact of there being two white girls among the Mohaves, and that these Yumas had stated that they were a part of a family who had been attacked, and some of them murdered, in 1851, by the Apaches. That the Apaches had since sold these girls to the Mohaves. "This letters" says Lorenzo, "I wet with my tears. I thought of that little Mary Ann, of the image that my last look into her face had left, and then of Olive. I began to reckon up their present age, and the years of dark captivity that had passed over them. Cani they yet be alive? May I yet see them? Will God help me?"

Lorenzo reached the Monte, after traveling all night, the next day about seven A. M. He saw Mr. Rowlit, and found the contents of the letter corroborated by him. He prepared a statement of the facts, and sent them to the "Los Angeles Star." These the editor published, kindly accompanying them by some well–timied and stirring remarks. This awakened an interest that the community had not felt before. While this was yet alive in the hearts and mouths of the people, a Mr. Black came into town, just from the East, by way of Fort Yuma. He stated that two girls were among the Mohaves, and that the chief had offered them to the officers at the fort for a mere nominal price, but that Commander Burke had refused to make the purchase. Of this statement Lorenzo knew nothing until he had seen it in the "Star." This threw a shade upon his mind, and gave him to think less of poor humanity than ever before. He found that but few placed any reliance upon the report. Mr. Bltek was well known in that vicinity, and those who knew him best were disposed to suspend judgment until the statement should be supported by other authority.

The editor of the "Star" had published the report with the best intentions, giving his authority. This report reached the fort, and created a great deal of sen sation. They sent the editor a letter denying the truthfiulness of the report, and requesting hinm to publish it, which he did. Accompanying the letter was a statement confirming the existence of a report at the fort of reliable intimations of the two girls being among the Mohaves, but that no offer had been made of delivering them up to the whites on any terms.

During this time Lorenzo had drawn up a petition, and obtained a large number of signers, praying of the Governor of California means and men to go and rescue his captive sisters. This was sent to Governor Johnson, at Sacramento, and the following reply was received:

"EXECUTIVE DEPARTMENT,
"SACRAMENTO, CAL., *Jan'y* 29, 1856.

"MR. LORENZO D. OATMAN. SIR,–A petition signed by yourself and numerous residents of the County of Los Angeles has been presented to me, asking assistance of 'men and means' to aid in the recovery of your sister, a captive among the Mohave tribe of Indians. It would afford me great pleasure, indeed, to render the desired assistance, were it in my power so to do. But by the constitution and laws of this state I have not the authority conferred on me to employ either 'men or means' to render this needful assistance; but will be most happy to cooperate in this laudable undertaking in any consistent way that may be presented. I would, however, suggest that through the general government the attention of the Indian Department being called to the subject, would more likely crown with success such efforts as might be necessary to employ in attempting the rescue of the unfortunate captive.

"Very respectfully your obedient servant,

"J. NIEELY JOHNSON."

Accordingly, and in accordance with the above suggestion, a preamble stating the facts, and a petition numerously signed, was drawn up and left at the office at the Steamer Landing to be forwarded to Washington. "Two days after," says Lorenzo, "I had resigned myself to patient waiting for a return of that petition, and went to work at some distance from the Monte in the woods."

He was still musing upon the one object of the last five years' solicitude. A new light had broken in upon his anxious heart. He had now some reliable information of the probable existence, though in a barbarous captivity, of those who were bound to him by the strongest ties.

He was left now to hope for their rescue, but not without painful fears lest something might yet intervene to prevent the realization of his new expectations. While thus engaged, alone and in the solitude of his thoughts, as well as of the wilderness, a friend rode up to him, and without speaking handed him a copy of the "Los Angeles Star," pointing at the same time to a notice contained in it. Hie opened it, and read as follows:

"An American Woman rescued fromn the Indians!—A woman, giving her name as Miss Olive Oatman, has been recently rescued from the Mohaves, and is now at Fort Yuma."

After getting this short note he took a horse and went immediately to Los Angeles. He went to the editor, and found that a letter had been received by him from Commander Burke, at Fort Yuma, stating that a young woman, calling herself "Olive Oatman," had been recently brought into the fort by a Yumna Indian, who had been rescued from the Mohave tribe; also stating to the editor that she had a brother who had lately been in this vicinity, and requesting the editor to give the earliest possible notice to that brother of the rescue of his sister. Lorenzo says:

"I requested him to let me see the letter, which he did. When I cainm.e to the facts contained in it concerning my sister, I could read no further; I was completely overcome. I laughed, I cried, I half doubted, I believed. It did not seem to be a reality. I now thought I saw a speedy realization, in part, of mny long–cherished hopes. I saw no mention of Mary Ann, and at once concluded that the first report obtained by way of Fort Yuma, by Yima Indians, was probably sadly true, that but one was alive. Too well founded were the fears I then had that poor Mary Ann had died among the savages, either by disease or cruelty.

"I was without money or means to get to the fort; but there were those who from the first had cherished a deep and active sympathy with me, and who were ready to do all in their power to aid me in my sorrow–strewn efforts for enslaved kindred.

"This same Mr. Low who had rode from Los Angeles to me near the Monte, kindly told me that he would assist me to obtain animals and get them ready for me, and that hlie would accompany me to Fort Yuma."

Thus outfitted, though not without much trembling and anxiety, questioning as to the certainty and reality of the reports, and of the rescued person really being his sister, yet feeling *it must be true;* with good hope he and Mr. Low were away early on the bright morning of the 10th of March for Fort Yuma, a distance of two hundred and fifty miles.

CHAPTER VII

Francisco goes over the River, and spends the Night–Persuades some of the Sub–Chiefs to apply again for Permission to let Olive go free His Threats–The Chiefs return with him–Secret Council–Another General Council–Danger of a Fight among themselves–Francisco has a Letter from the Whites–Olive present–Francisco gains Per mission to give her the Letter–Its Contents–Much alarmed Speeches of the Indians–Advice to kill their Captive–Determine to release her–Daughter of tihe Chief goes with them–Their Journey–At Fort Yuma.

For a long time Olive had been apprised of the fact that intercourse had been kept up between the Mohaves and the whites, as articles had been brought in, from time to time, that she knew must have been obtained from white settlements, either by plunder or purchase. These were brought in by small parties, one of whom would frequently be absent several days or weeks at a time.

She saw in these the evidences that she was within reach still of the race to which she belonged; and often would gaze with interest and curiosity upon some old tattered garment that had been brought in, until the remembrances and associations it would awaken would bring tears and sighs to end the bitter meditations upon that brighter and happier people, now no longer hers. She ventured to ask questions concerning these trips, and the place where they found the whites; but all her anxious queries were met by threats and taunts, or a long, gibberish dissertation upon the perfidy of the whites, india–rubber stories upon the long distance of the whites away, or a restatement of their malignant hate toward them, and of their purpose to use the knowledge they might gain by these professed friendly visits to their ultimate overthrow, by treachery and deceit. They even professed to disbelieve the statements that had so long deceived them concerning the numerical strength of the whites, and to believe that the few of them yet remaining could and would be overcome and extinguished by the combined power of the Indian tribes, that at no distant day would be directed against them.

The chief's daughter, however, ventured to tell Olive, under injunction of secrecy, that some of their number knew well and had frequently traversed the road leading to white settlements; but that it was an immense distance, and that none but Indians could find it; besides that it was guarded by vigilant spies against the incoming of ally but their own race.

It should be kept in mind that as yet Olive had been forbidden a word with Francisco. We left the narrative of Olive, in another chapter, involved in the heated and angry debates of a long and tedious council. Upon that wild council she had been waiting in dreadful suspense, not a little mingled with terrible forebodings of her own personal safety. This convention came to a conclusion with a positive and peremptory refusal to liberate the captive; and a resolution to send Francisco away, under injunction not again under penalty of torture, to revisit their camp. Francisco, on the same night, departed to the other side of the river; the chiefs and sub–chiefs dispersed, and Olive was left to her own melancholy musings over the probable result.

She now began to regret that anything had been said or done about her rescue. She was in darkness as to the effect that all this new excitement upon her stay among them might have, after it should become a matter of sober deliberation by the Mohaves alone. She saw and heard enough, directly and indirectly, to know that they were set upon not letting her go free. She began to fear for her life, especially as she saw the marked changes in the conduct of the Indians toward her. The wife of the chief seemed to feel kind still toward her; but yet she plainly evinced that the doings of the last few days had compelled her to disguise her real feelings. The chief was changed from a pleasant don't–care spectator of Olive's situation, to a sullen, haughty, overbearing tyrant and oppressor.

Olive was now shut up to a newly enkindled hate, which sought opportunities to ftiume its wrath against her. She now regarded all efforts for her rescue as having reached a final and abrupt close. But still she could not be ignorant, concealed and reserved as they were in all their mutual consultations, of the fact that some dreadful fear for themselves was galling and tormenting them. Expressions that she well understood, and conveying their dread of the whites, and fear that they might execute the threats brought by Francisco, constantly escaped them, and came to the ears of the agitated subject and victim of their new rage.

Francisco spent the night upon which the council closed across the river. He there plied every argument and stratagem that his cunning mind could devise to persuade the principal men on that side of the Colorado to recede from the resolution they had that day reached.–Hie employed the whole night in setting before them troubles that these rash resolutions would bring upon them, and to convince them that it was for their sakes alone that he desired to bear the captive to the fort with him.

He had resolved in his own mind not to leave without her, as she afterward learned; and, on the failure of all other means, to risk his life in a bold attempt to steal her away under darkness of night. But in the morning he made preparations for leaving, (he really intended to go back to the village,) when the magnates and councilmen, among whom he had tarried for the night, came to him, and prevailed upon him to go back with them, promising him that they had now determined to do all in their power to persuade the chief and tribe to yield to his demand, and to let the captive go; fearing for the result to themselves of the contrary determination already reached.

About noon of the next day Olive saw Francisco, with a large number of Mohaves, come into the village. It was not without much fear and alarm that she saw this, though such had been the intense anxiety about her situation, and the possibility of escape that the last few days had enkindled, she felt willing to have a final conclusion now formed, whether it should be her death or release.

To live much longer there, she now thought she plainly saw would be impossible; as she could only expect to be sold or barbarously dispatched, after all that had passed upon the question of her release. Besides this she felt that with the knowledge she had now gained of the nearness and feeling of the whites, it would be worse than death to be doomed to the miseries of her captivity, almost in sight of the privileges of her native land. And hence, though the reappearance of Francisco was an occasion for new tumult, and her own agitation intense, she felt comforted in the prospect it opened of ending the period of her present living death.

"When Francisco returned I was out gathering ottileka, (a small ground–nut of the size of the hazelnut,) and had utterly abandoned the hope of being released, as the council had broken up with an utter refusal to let me go. Had I known all that had transpired I should have felt much worse than as it was. I learned from Francisco since, that the Indians had resolved (those who were friendly to my going) that for fear that the whites would come to rescue me, they would kill me as soon as it was decided I should not go.

"I had not as yet seen the letter that Francisco brought to me. I plainly saw a change in the conduct of the Indians to me since the close of the recent agitation. What it foretold I could not even conjecture. But I saw enough before swinging my basket that morning upon my back to go out digging ottileka, to convince me that the wrath of many of them was aroused. I struggled to suppress any emotion I felt, while my anxious heart was beating over possible dreaded results of this kind attempt to rescue me, which I thought I saw were to be of a very different character from those intended."

The returning company came immediately to the house of the chief. At first the chief refused to receive them. After a short secret council with some members of his cabinet, he yielded; the other chiefs were called, and with Francisco they were again packed in council. The criers were again hurried forth, and the tribe was again convened.

At this council Olive was permitted to remain. The speaking was conducted with a great deal of confusion, which the chief found it difficult to

Olive at the Indian Council

prevent; speakers were frequently interrupted, and at times there was a wild, uproarious tumult, and a Heated temper and heated speech were the order of the day. Says Olive:

"It did seem during that night, at several stages of the debate, that there was no way of preventing a general fight among them. Speeches were made, which, judging from their gestures and motions, as well as from what I could understand in their heat and rapidity, were full of the most impassioned elo quence.

"I found that they had told Francisco that I was not an American, that I was from a race of people mtch like the Indians, living away to the setting sun. They had painted my face, and feet, and hands of a dun, dingy color, unlike that of any race I ever saw. This they told me they did to deceive Francisco; and that I must not talk to him in American. They told me to talk to him in another language, and to tell him that I was not an American. They then waited to hear the result, expecting to hear my gibberish nonsense, and to witness the convincing effect upon Francisco. But I spoke to him in broken English, and told him the truth, and also what they had enjoined me to do. He started from his seat in a perfeet rage, vowing that he would be imposed upon no longer. He then broke forth upon them with one of the most vehement addresses I ever heard. I felt and still feel an anxiety to know the full contents of that speech. Part of it he gave me on the way to the fort. It was full of eloquence, and was an exhibition of talent rarely found among his race.

"The Mohave warriors threatened to take my life for disobeying their orders. They were doubly chagrinied that their scheme had failed, and also that their dishonest pretensions of my unwillingness to go with him, and of my not being an American, had been found out. Some of them persisted still in the falsehood, saying that I had learned some American froti living among them, but that I had told them that I was not of that race. All this transpired after Francisco's return, and during his second and last effort for my rescue.

"I narrowly looked at Francisco, and soon found he was one whom I had seen there before, and who had tarried with the chief about three months previously. I sflw he held a letter in his hand and asked to let me see it. Toward morning it was handed me, and Francisco told me it was from the Americans. I took it, and after a little made out the writing on the outside.

"'FRANCISCO, A YUMA INDIAN, GOING TO THE MOHAVES.'

'I opened it with much agitation. All was quiet as the drove around me. I examined it for a long time ere I could get the sense, having seen no writing for five years. It was as follows:

"'FRANCISCO, Yuma Indian, bearer of this, goes to the Mohave Nation to obtain a white woman there, named OLIVIA. It is desirable she should come to this post, or send her reasons why she does no wish to come.

MARTIN BURKE.
Lieut. Col., Commanding.

HEAD–QUARTERS, FORT YUMA, CAL.,
27th January, 1856.'

"They now began to importune and threaten me to give them the contents of the letter. I waited and meditated for some time. I did not know whether it was best to give it to them just as it was. Up to this time I had striven to manifest no anxiety about the matter. They had questioned and teased with every art, from little children up to men, to know my feelings, though they should have known them well by this time. I dared not in the excitement express a wish. Francisco had told them that the whites knew where I was, and that they were about armiing a sufficient number to surround the whole Indian nations, and that they thus intended to destroy them all unless they gave up the last captive among them. He told them that the men at the fort would kill himself and all they could find of them with the Yumas, if he should not bring her back. He said it was out of mercy to his own tribe, and to them that he had come.

"They were still pressing me to read them the letter. I then told them what was in it, and also that the Americans would send a large army and destroy the Yumas and Mohaves, with all the Indians they could find, unless I should return with Franscisco. I never expect to address so attentive an audience again as I did then.

"I found that they had been representing to Francisco that I did not wish to go to the whites. As soon as they thought they had the contents of the letter, there was the breaking out of scores of voices at once, and our chief found it a troublesome meeting to preside over. Some advised that I should be killed, and that Francisco should report that I was dead. Others that they at once refuse to let me go, and that the whites could not hurt them. Others were in favor of letting me go at once. And it was not until daylight that one could judge which counsel would prevail.

"In all this Francisco seemed bold, calm, and determined. He would answer their questions and objections with the tact and cunning of a pure Indian.

"It would be impossible to describe my own feelings on reading that letter, and during the remainder of the pow–wow. I saw now a reality in all that was said and done. There was the handwriting of one of my own people, and the whole showed plainly that my situation was known, and that there was a purpose to secure my return. I sought to keep my emotions to myself, for fear of the effect it might have upon my doom, to express a wish or desire."

During this time the captive girl could only remain in the profoundest and most painful silence, though *the one* of all the agitated crowd most interested in the matter and result of the debate. Daylight came slowly up the east, finding the assembly still discussing the life and death question (for such it really was) that had called them together.

Some time after sunrise, and after Francisco and the captive had been bid retire, the chief called them again in, and told them, with much reluctance, that the decision had been to let the captive go.

"At this," says Olive, "and while yet in their presence, I found I could no longer control my feelings, and I burst into tears, no longer able to deny myself the pleasure of thus expressing the weight of feeling that struggled for relief and utterance within me.

"I found that it had been pleaded against my being given up, that Francisco was suspected of simply coming to get me away from the Mohaves that I might be retained by the Yumas. The chief accused him of this, and said he believed it. This excited the anger of Francisco, and he boldly told them what he thought of them, and told them to go with their captive; that they would sorrow for it in the end. When it was determined that I might go; the chief said that his daughter should go and see that I was carried to the whites. We ate our breakfast, supplied ourselves with mushed musquite, and started. Three Yuma Indian's had come with Francisco, to accompany him to and from the Mohaves; his brother and two cousins.

"I now began to think of really leaving my Indian home. Involuntarily my eye strayed over that valley. I gazed on every familiar object. The mountains that stood about our valley home, like sentinels tall and bold, their every shape, color, and height, as familiar as the door–yard about the dwelling in which I had been reared.

"Again my emotions were distrusted, and I could hardly believe that what was passing was reality. 'Is it true,' I asked, 'that they have concluded to let me escape? I fear they will change their mind. Can it be that I am to look upon the white face again?' I then felt like hastening as for my life, ere they could revoke their decision. Their looks, their motions, their flashing eyes reminded me that I was not out of danger. Some of them came to me and sillily laughed, as much as to say: 'O, you feel very finely now, don't you?' Others stood and gazed upon me with a steady, serious look, as if taking more interest in my welfare than ever before. More than this I seemed to read in their singular appearance; they seemed to stand in wonder as to where I could be going. Some of them seemed to feel a true joy that I was made so happy, and they would speak to me to that effect.

"One little incident took place on the morning of my departure, that clearly reflects the littleness and meanness that inheres in the general character of the

Indian. I had several small strings of beads; most of them had been given me for singing to them when requested, when they had visitors from other tribes. I purposed at once that I would take these beads, together with some small pieces of blankets that I had obtained at different times, and was wearing upon my person at this time, to the whites as remembrancers of the past; but when I was about ready to start, the son of the chief camne and took all my beads, with every woolen shred he could find about me, and quietly told me that I could not take them with me. This, though a comparatively trifling matter, afflicted me. I found that I prized those beads beyond their real value; especially one string that had been worn by Mary. I had hoped to retain them while I might live. I then gathered up a few small ground–nuts, which I had dug with my own hanlds, and concealed them; and some of them I still keep."

That same kind daughter of the chief who had so often in suppressed and shy utterances spoken the word of condolence, and the wish to see Olive sent to her native land, and had given every possible evidence of a true and unaffected desire for her welfare, she was not sorry to learn was to attend her upon the long and tedious trip by which her reunion with the whites was hoped to be reached.

But there was one spot in that valley of captivity that possessed a mournful attraction for the emancipated captive. Near the wigwam where she had spent many hours in loneliness, and Indian converse with her captors, was a mound that marked the final resting–place of her last deceased sister. Gladly would she, if it had been in her power, have gathered the few–moldering remains of that loved and cherished form, and borne them away to a resting–place on some shaded retreat in the soil of her own countrymen. But this privilege was denied her, and that too while she knew that immediately upon her exit they would probably carry their already made threats of burning them into execution. And who would have left such a place, so enshrined in the heart as that must have been, without a struggle, though her way fiom it lay toward the home of the white man? That grave upon which she had so often knelt, and upon which she had so often shed the bitter tear, the only place around which affection lingered, must now be abandoned; not to remain a place for the undisturbed repose of her sister's remains, but to disgorge its precious trust in obedience to the rude, barbarous superstition that had waved its custom at the time of her death. No wonder that she says: " I went to the grave of Mary Ann, and took a last look of the little mound marking the resting–place of my sister who had come with me to that lonely exile; and now I felt what it was to know she could not go with rme from it."

There had been in the employ of government at Fort Yuma, since 1853, a Mr. Grinell, known, from his occupation, by the name of Carpenteio. He was a man of a large heart, and of many excellent qualities. He was a man who never aimed to put on an exte rior to his conduct that could give any deceptive impression of heart and character. Indeed he often presented a roughness and uncouthness which, how ever repulsive to the stranger, was found in ever the less, on an acquaintance, to cover a noble nature of large and generous impulses. A man of diligence and fidelity, he merited and won the confidence of all who knew him. He possessed a heart that could enter into sympathy with the subjects of suffering wherever he found them. Soon after coming to Fort Yuma, he had learned of the fate of the Oatman family, and of the certainty of the captivity of two of the girls. With all the eagerness and solicitude that could be expected of a kinsman, he inquired diligently into the particulars, and also the reliability of the current statements concerning these unfortunate captives. Nor did these cease in a moment or a day.

He kept up a vigilant outsight, searching to glean, if possible, something by which to reach definite knowledge of them. He was friendly to the Yumas, numbers of whom were constantly about the fort. Of them he inquired frequently and closely. Among those with whomn he was most familiar, and who was in most favor among the officers at the fort, was Francisco. Carpentero had about given up the hope of accomplishing what he desired, when one night Francisco crept by some means through the guard, and found his way into the tent of his fiend, long after he had retired.

Grinell awoke, and in alarm drew his pistol and demanded who was there. Francisco spoke, and his voice was known. Grinell asked him what he could be there for at that hour of the night. With an air of indifference he said he had only come in to talk a little. After a long silence and some suspicious movements, he broke out and said: "Carpentero, what is this you say so much about two Amer–icanos among the Indians?"

"Said," replied Grinell; "I said that there are two girls among the Mohaves or Apaches, and you know it, and we know that you know it." Grinell then took up a copy of the Los Angeles Star, and told Francisco to listen, and he would read him what the Americans were saying and thinking about it. He then reads, giving the interpretation in Mexican, (which language Francisco could speak fluently,) an article that had been gotten up and published at the instance of Lorenzo, containing the report brought in by Mr. Rowlit, calling for help. The article also stated that a large number of men were ready to undertake to rescue the captives at once, if means could be furnished.

But the quick and eager mind of Carpentero did not suffer the article to stop with what he could find in the Star; keeping his eye still upon the paper, he continued to read, that if the captives were not delivered in so many days, there would be five millions of men thrown around the mountains inhabited by the Indians, and that they would annihilate the last one of them, if they did not give up all the white captives.

Many other things did that Star tell at that time, of a like import, but the which had got into the paper (if there at all) without editor, type, or ink.

Francisco listened with mouth, and ears, and eyes. After a short silence, he said, (in Mexican,) "I know where there is one white girl among the Mohaves; there were two, but one is dead."

At this the generous heart of Carpentero began to swell, and the object of his anxious, disinterested sympathy for the first time began to present itself as a bright reality.

"When did you find out she was there?" said Carpentero.

F. "I have just found it out to–night."

C. "Did you not know it before?"

F. "Well, not long; me just come in, you know. Me know now she is there among the Mohaves."

Carpentero was not yet fully satisfied that all was right. There had been, and still was, apprehension of some trouble at the fort, from the Yumas; and Carpentero did not know but that some murderous scheme was concocted, and all this was a ruse to beguile and deceive them.

Carpentero then told Francisco to stay in his tent for the night. Francisco then told Carpentero that if Commander Burke would give him autlhority, he would go and bring the girl into the fort. That night Carpentero slept awake. Early in the morning they went to the commander. For some time Commander Burke was disposed to regard it as something originated by the cunning of Francisco, and did not believe hlie would bring the girl in. Said Francisco: "You give me four blankets and some beads, and I will bring her in just twenty days, when the sun be right over here," pointing to about forty–five degrees above the western horizon.

Carpentero begged the captain to place all that it would cost for the outfit to his own account, and let him go. The captain consented, a letter was written, and the Yuma, with a brother and two others, started. This was about the eighth of February, 1856.

Several days passed, and the men about the fort thought they had Carpentero in a place where it would do to remind him of "his trusty Francisco." And thus they did, asking him if he "did not think his blankets and beads had sold cheap?" if he'"had not better send another Indian after the blankets?" etc., with other questions indicating their own distrust of the whole movement.

On the twentieth day, about noon, three Yuma Indians, living some distance from the fort, came to the fort and asked permission to see "a man by the name of Carpentero." They were shown–his tenlt, and went in and made themselves known, saying, " Carpentero, Francisco is coming."

"Has he the girl with him?" quickly asked the agitated Carpentero, bounding to his feet.

They laughed sillily, saying, "Francisco will come here when the slin be right over there," pointing in the direction marked by Francisco.

With eager eyes Carpentero stood gazing for some time, when three Indians and two females, dressed in closely woven bark skirts, came down to the ferry on the opposite side of the river. At that he bounded toward them, crying at the top of his voice, "They have come; *the captive girl is here!"* All about the fort were soon apprised that it was even so, and soon they were either running to meet and welcome the captive, or were gazing with eagerness to know if this strange report could be true.

Olive, with her characteristic modesty, was unwilling to appear in her bark attire and her poor shabby dress among the whites, eager as she was to catch again a glimpse of their countenances, one of whom she had not seen for years. As soon as this was made known, a noble–hearted woman, the wife of one of the officers and the lady to whose kind hospitalities she was afterward indebted for every kindness that could minister to her comfort the few weeks she tarried there, sent her a dress and clothing of the best she had.

Amid long enthusiastic cheering and the booming of cannon, Miss Olive was presented to the commander of the fort by Francisco. Every one seemed to partake of the joy and enthusiasm that prevailed. Those who had been the most skeptical of the intentions of Francisco, were glad to find their distrust rebuked in so agreeable a manner. The Yumas gathered in large numbers, and seemed to partake in the general rejoicing, joining their heavy shrill voices in the shout, and fairly mnaking the earth tremble beneath the thunder of their cheering.

Francisco told the captain he had been compelled to give more for the captive than what he had obtained of him; that he had promised the Mohave chief a horse, and that his daughter was now present to see that this promise was fulfilled. Also, that a son of the chief would be in within a few days to receive the horse. A good horse was given him, and each of the kind officers at the fort testified their gratitude to him, as well as their hearty sympathy with the long separated brother and sister, by donating freely and liberally of their money to make up a horse for Francisco; and he was told there, in the presence of the rest of his tribe, that he had not only performed an act for which the gratitude of the whites would follow him, but one that might probably save his tribe and the Mohaves much trouble and many lives.

From this Francisco was promoted and became a "Tie" of his tribe, and with characteristic pride and haughtiness of bearing, showed the capabilities of the Indian to appreciate honors and preferment, by looking with disdain and contempt upon his peers, and treating them thus in the presence of the whites.

Miss Olive was taken in by a very excellent family residing at the fort at the time, and every kindness and tender regard bestowed upon her that her

ARRIVAL OF OLIVE AT FORT YUMA

generous host and hostess could make minister to her contentment and conmfort. She had come over three hundred and fifty miles during the last ten days; frequently (as many as ten times) she and her guides were compelled to swim the swollen streams, running and rushing to the top of their banks with ice–water. The kind daughter of the chief, with an affection that had increased with every month and year of their association, showed more concern and eagerness for the wellbeing of "Olivia" than her own. She would carry, through the long and toilsome day, the roll of blankets that they shared together during the night, and seemed very much concerned and anxious lest somethiing might yet prevent her safe arrival at the place of destination.

Olive was soon apprised of the place of residence of her brother, whom she had so long regarded as dead, and also of his untiring efforts, during the last few years, for the rescue of his sister.

"It was some time," she says, "before I could realize that he was yet alive. The last time I saw him he was dragged in his own blood to the rocks upon the brow of that precipice; I thought I knew him to be dead." And it was not until all the circumstances of his escape were detailed to her that she could fully credit his rescue and preservation. Lorenzo and his trading companion, Mr. Low, were about ten days in reaching the fort; each step and hour of that long and dangerous journey his mind was haunted by the fear that the rescued girl might not be his sister. But he had not been long at the fort ere his trembling heart was made glad by the attestation of his own eyes to the reality He saw that it was his own sister (the same, though now grown and much changed) who, with Mary Ann, had poured their bitter cries upon his bewildered senses five years before, as they were hurried away by the unheeding Apaches, leaving him for dead with the rest of the family.

Language was not made to give utterance to the feelings that rise, and swell, and throb through the human bosom upon such a meeting as this. For five years they had not looked in each other's eyes; the last image of that brother pressed upon the eye and mnemory of his affectionate sister, was one that could only make any reference to it in her mind one of painful, torturing horror. She had seen him when (as she supposed) life had departed, dragged in the most inhuman manner to one side; one of a whole family who had been butchered before her eyes. The last remembrance of that sister by her brother, was of her wailings and heart–rending sighs over the massacre of the rest of her family, and her consign ment to a barbarous captivity or torturing death. She was grown to womanhood; she was changed, but despite the written traces of her outdoor life and barbarous treatment left upon her appearance and person, he could read the assuring evidences of her family identity. They met, they wept, they em braced each other in the tenderest manner; heart throbbed to heart, and pulse beat to pulse; but for nearly one hour not one word could either speak! The past! the checkered past! with its bright and its dark, its sorrow and its joy, rested upon that hour of speechless joy. The season of bright childhood, their mutual toils and anxieties of nearly one year, while traveling over that gloomy way; that horrid night of massacre, with its wailing and praying, mingled with fiendish whooping and yelling, remeinmbered in connection with its rude separation; the five years of tears, loneliness, and captivity among savag,es, through which she had grown up to womanhood; the same period of his captivity to the dominion of a harassing anxiety and solicitude, through which he had grown up to manhood, all pressed upon the time of that meeting, to choke utterance, and stir the soul with emotions that could only pour themselves out in tears and sighs.

A large company of Americans, Indians, and Mexicans, were present and witnessed the meeting of Lorenzo and his sister. Some of them are now in the city of San Francisco, to testify that not an unmoved heart nor a dry eye witnessed it. Even the rude and untutored Indian, raised his brawny hand to wipe away the unbidden tear that stole upon his cheek as he stood speechless and wonder–struck! When the feelings became controllable, and words came to their relief, they dwelt and discoursed for hours upon the gloomy and pain–writtenl past. In a few days they were safe at the Montĕ, and were there met by a cousin from Rogue River Valley, Oregon, who had heard of the rescue of Olive, and had come to take her to his own home.

At the Montĕ they were visited during a stay of two weeks, in waiting for the steamer, by large numbers of people, who bestowed upon the rescued captive all possible manifestations of interest in her welfare, and hearty rejoicing at her escape from the night of prison–life and suffering so long endured.

She was taken to Jackson County, Oregon, where she has been since, and is still residing there.

Since writing the above Miss Oatman, with her brother, have spent about six months at school in Santa Clara Valley, California. On the fifth day of March, 1858, they left San Francisco, in company with the writer and his family, on the steamship Golden Age, for New–York, where they arrived on the 26th of the same month.

Lorenzo Oatman.

CONCLUSION

How strangc the life of these savages. Of their past history how little is known; and there is an utter destitution of any reliable data upon which to conjecture even concerning it. By some they are considered the descendants of a people who were refined and enlightened. That a period of civilization, and of some progress in the arts, preceded the discovery of this continent by Columbus, there can be but little doubt. The evidences of this are to be seen in the relics of buried cities and towns, that have been found deep under ground in numerous places.

But whether the people of whom we have these traces extended to the Pacific slope, and to the southwest, we know not. This much we do know: there are large tracts of country now occupied by large and numerous tribes of the red race, living in all the filth and degradation of an unmitigated heathenism, and without any settled systemn of laws or social regulations.

If they have any system of government, it is that of an absolute monarchy. The chief of each tribe is the sole head and sovereign in all matters that affect the wellbeing of the same, even to the life and death of its members.

They are human, but live like brutes. They seem totally destitute of all those noble and generous traits of life which distinguish and honor civilized people. In indolence and supineness they seem content to pass their days, without ambition, save of war and conquest; they live the mere creatures of passion, blind and callous to all those ennobling aims and purposes that are the true and pleasing inspiration of rational existence. In their social state, the more they are studied the more do they become an object of disgust and loathing.

They manifest but little affection for one another, only when death has separated them, and then they show the deep inhumanity and abject heathenism to which they have sunk by the horrid rites that prevail in the disposing of their infirm kindred and their dead. They burn the one and the other with equal impunity and satisfaction.

The marriage relation among them is not honored, scarcely observed. The least affront justifies the husband in casting off his chosen wife, and even in taking her life. Rapine and lust prey upon them at home; and war is fast wasting them abroad. They regard the whites as enemies from all antiquity, and any real injury they can do them is considered a virtue, while the taking of their lives (especially of males) is an act which is suire to crown the name of the perpetrator with eternal honors.

With all their boasting and professed contempt for the whites, and with all their bright traditions and prophecies, according to which their day of triumph and power is near at hand, yet they are not without premonitions of a sad and fatal destiny. They are generally dejected and cast down; the tone of their every–day life, as well as sometimes actual sayings, indicating a pressing fear and harassing foreboding.

Some of the females would, after hours of conlversation with Olive, upon the character, customs, and prosperity of the whites, plainly, but with injunctions of secrecy, tell her that they lived in constant fear; and it was not unfrequent that some disaffected mr.ember of the tribe would threaten to leave his mountain home and go to live with the whites. It is not to be understood that this was the prevailing state of feeling among them.

Most of them are sunk in an ignorance that forbids any aspiration or ambition to reach or fire their natures; an ignorance that knows no higher mode of life than theirs, and that looks with jealousy upon every nation and people, save the burrowing tribes that skulk and crawl among these mountains and ravines.

But fate seems descending upon them, if not in "sudden," yet in certain night. They are waning. Remnants of them will no doubt long survive; but the masses of them seem fated to a speedy decay. Since this narrative was first written, a very severe battle, lasting several weeks, has taken place between the allied Mohaves and Yumas on the one side, and the Cochopas on the other. The former lost over three hundred warriors; the latter but few, less than threescore. Among the slain was the noble Francisco. It is rumored at Fort Yuma, that during the engagement the allied tribes were informed by their oracles that their ill–success was owing to Francisco; that he must be slain for his firiendship to the whites; then victory would crown their struggles; and that, in obedience to this superstition, he was slain by the hands of his own tribe.

Had Olive been among them during this unsuccessful war, her life would have been offered up on the return of the defeated warriors; and no doubt there were then many among them who attributed their defeat to the conciliation on their part by which she was surrendered to her own people. Such is the Indian of the South and Southwest.

We have tried to give the reader a correct, though brief history of the singular and strange fate of that unfortunate family. If there is one who shall be disposed to regard the reality as overdrawn, we have only to say that every fact has been dictated by word of mouth fi'om the surviving members of that once happy family, who have, by a mysterious Providence, after suffering a prolonged and unrelieved woe of five years, been rescued and again restored to the blessings of a civilized and sympathizing society.

Most of the preceding pages have been written in the first person. This method was adopted for the sake of brevity, as also to give, as near as language may do it, a faithful record of the feeling8 and spirit with which the distresses and cruel treatment of the few years over which these pages run, was met, braved, endured, and triumphed over. The record of the five years of captivity cntered upon by a timid, inexperienced girl of fourteen years, and during which, associated with naught but savage life, she grew up to womanhood, presents one of heroism, self–possession, and patience, that might do honor to one of maturity and years. Much of that dreadful period is unwritten, and will remain forever unwritten.

We have confidence that every reader will share with us the feelings of gratitude to Almighty God for the blessings of civilization, and a superior social life, with which we cease to pen this record of the degradation, the barbarity, the superstition, the squalidness, that curse the uncounted thousands who people the caverns and wilds that divide the Eastern from the Western inheritance of our mother republic.

But the unpiereed heathenism that thus stretches its wing of night upon these swarming mountains and vales, is not long to have a dominion so wild, nor possess victims so numerous. Its territory is already begirt with the light of a higher life; and now the foot–fall of the pioneering, brave Anglo Saxon is heard upon the heel of the savage, and breaks the silence along his winding trail. Already the song and shout of civilization wakes echoes long and prophetic upon those mountain rocks, that have for centuries hemmed in an unvisited savageness.

Until his death Francisco, by whose vigilance the place of Olive's captivity and suffering was ascertained, and who dared to bargain for her release and restoration ere he had changed a word with her captors about it, was hunted by his own and other tribes for guiding the white man to the hiding–places of those whose ignorance will not suffer them to let go their filth and superstition, and who regard the whole transaction as the opening of the door to the greedy, aggressive, white race. The cry of gold, like that which formed and matured a state upon this far–off coast in a few years, is heard along ravines that have been so long exclusively theirs, and companies of gold hunters, led on by faint but unerring "prospects," are confidently seeking rich leads of the precious ore near their long isolated wigwams.

The march of American civilization, if unhampered by the weakness and corruption of its own happy subjects, will yet, and soon, break upon the barbarity of these numerous tribes, and either elevate them to the unappreciated blessings of a superior state, or wipe them into oblivion, and give their long–unde veloped territory to another.

Perhaps when the intricate and complicated events that mark and pave the way to this state of things, shall be pondered by the curious and retrospective eye of those who shall rejoice in its possession, these comparatively insignificant ones spread out for the reader upon these pages, will be found to form a part. May Heaven guide the anxious–freighted future to the greatest good of the abject heathen, and save those into whose hands are committed such openings and privileges for beneficent doing, from the perversion of their blessings and mission.

"Honor to whom honor is due." With all the degradation in which these untamed hordes are steeped, there are–strange as it may seem–some traits and phases in their conduct which, on comparison with those of some who call themselves civilized, ought to crimson their cheeks with a blush. While feuds have been kindled, and lives have been lost–innocent lives–by the intrusion of the white man upon the domestic relations of Indian families; while decency and chastity have been outraged, and the Indian female, in some instances, stolen from her spouse and husband that she really loved; let it be written, written if possible so as to be read when an inscrutable but unerring Providence shall exact "to the uttermost farthing" for every deed of cruelty and lust perpetrated by a superior race upon an inferior one; *written* to stand out before those whose duty and position it shall be, within a few years, in the American Council of State, to deliberate and legislate upon the best method to dispose of these fast waning tribes; that *one of our own race, in tender years, committed wholly to their power, assed a five-years' captivity among these savages withtout falling under those baser propensities which ralve, and rage, and eonsume, wi(th the fury and fatality of a pestilence, amony themselves.*

It is true that their uncultivated and untempered traditional superstitions allow them to mark in the white man an enemy that has preyed upon their rights from antiquity, and to exact of him, when thrown into their power, cruelties that kindle just horror in the breast of the refined and the civilized. It is true that the more intelligent, and the large majority, deplore the poor representation of our people that has been given to these wild men by certain "lewd fellows of the baser sort," who are undistinguished by them from our race as a whole. But they are set down to our account in a more infallible record than any of mere human writ; and delicate and terrible is the responsibility with which they have clothed the action of the American race amid the startling and important exigences that must roll upon its pathway for the next few years.

Who that looks at the superstition, the mangled, fragmentary, and distorted traditions that form the only tribunal of appeal for the little *wreck of mnoral sense* they have left themn–superstitions that hold them as with the grasp of omnipotence; who that looks upon the self–consuming workings of the corruptions that breed in the hotbed of ignorance, can be so hardened that his heart has no sigh to heave, no groan to uter over a social, moral, and political desolation that ought to appeal to our commniseration rather than put a torch to our slumbering vengeance.

It is true that this coast and the Eastern states have now their scores of lonely wanderers, mournful and sorrow–stricken mourners, over whose sky has been cast a mantle of gloom that will stretch to their tombs for the loss of those of their kindred who sleep in the dust, or bleach upon the sand–plots trodden by these roaming heathen; kindred who have in their innocence fallen by cruelty. But there is a voice coming up from these scattered, unmonumented resting–places of their dead; and it pleads, pleads with the potency and unerringliess of those pleadings from "under the ground" of ancient date, and of the fact and effect of which we have a guiding record.

Who that casts his eye over the vast territory that lies between the Columbia River and Acapulco, with the Rocky Range for its eastern bulwark, a territory abounding with rich verdure–clad vales and pasturage hill–sides, and looks to the time, not distant, when over it all shall be spread the wing of the eagle, when the music of civilization, of the arts, of the sciences, of the mechanismn, of the religion of our favored race, shall roll along its winding rivers and over its beautiful slopes, but has one prayer to offer to the God of his fathers, that the same wisdom craved and received by them to plant his civil light–house on a wilderness shore, may still guide us on to a glorious, a happy, and a useful destiny.

The following lines were written by some person, unknown to the author, residing in Maysville, California. They were first published in a daily paper, soon after the first edition was issued. They are here inserted as expressing, not what one merely, but what many felt who read this narrative in that state, and who have become personally acquainted with Miss Oatman. Many have been the assurances of sympathy and affection that, by letter and in person, have been in kindred and equally fervent strains poured upon the ear and heart of the once suffering subject of this narrative.

STANZAS TO OLIVE OATMAN

Fair Olive! thy historian's pen declines
Portraying what thy feelings once have been,
Because the language of the world confines
Expression, giving only half we mean;
No reaching from what we have felt or seen:
And it is well. How useless'tis to gild
Refinbd gold, or paint the lily's sheen!
But we can weep when all the heart is fill'd
And feel in thought, beyond where pen or words are skill'd.

In moonlight we can fancy that one grave,
Resting amid the mountains bleak and bare,
Although no willow's swinging pendants wave
Above the little captive sleeping there,
With thee beside her wrapp'd in voiceless prayer;
We guess thy anguish, feel thy heart's deep woe,
And list for moans upon the midnight air,
As tears of sympathy in silence flow
For her whose unmark'd head is lying calm and low.

For in the bosom of the wilderness
Imagination paints a fearful wild
With two young children bow'd in deep distress,
A simple maiden and a little child,
Begirt with savages in circles fill'd,
Who round them shout in triumph o'er the deed
That laid their kindred on the desert piled
An undistinguished mass, in death to bleed,
And left them without hope in their despairing need.

In captive chains whole races have been led,
But never yet upon one heart did fall
Misfortune's hand so heavy. Thy young head
Has born a nation's griefs, its woes, and all
The serried sorrows which earth's histories call
The hand of God. Then, Olive, bend thy knee,
Morning and night, until the funeral pall
Hides thy fair face to Him who watches thee,
Whose power once made thee bond, whose power once set thee free.

MONTBAR.

MARYSVILLE, *April 27,* 1857.